last summer

REBECCA A. ROGERS

Dear Reader,

As I wrote this book, I couldn't help but think about the many people across the world affected by drug addiction. So many times we believe it won't happen to us, but the truth of the matter is, at some point in our lives, we'll know someone who is battling an addiction, whether it's drugs, alcohol, or otherwise. Here are some statistics according to the National Institute on Drug Abuse for 2009 (there are various updated studies on NIDA's website, as shown in number eight below, but this was the last full survey conducted by NIDA):

1. 605,000 Americans age 12 and older had abused heroin at least once in the year prior to being surveyed.

2. 51.9% of Americans age 12 or older had used alcohol at least once in the 30 days prior to the survey.

3. 4.8 million Americans age 12 or older had abused cocaine in any form, and 1.0 million had abused crack at least once in the year prior to being surveyed.

4. 779,000 Americans age 12 or older had abused LSD (Acid) at least once in the year prior to being surveyed.

5. 28.5 million Americans age 12 or older had abused marijuana at least once in the year prior to being surveyed.

6. 2.8 million Americans age 12 or older had abused MDMA (Ecstasy) at least once in the year prior to being surveyed.

7. 16 million Americans age 12 and older had taken a prescription pain reliever, tranquilizer, stimulant, or sedative for nonmedical purposes at least once in the year prior to being surveyed.

8. The NIDA-funded 2010 Monitoring the Future Study showed that 0.5% of 8th graders, 1.0% of 10th graders, and 1.5% of 12th graders had abused anabolic steroids at least once in the

year prior to being surveyed.

If you or someone you love is suffering from an addiction, there's still hope. There are a number of treatment options, but they each start with you. For residents of the United States, you can contact the National Institute on Drug Abuse (NIDA) at 1-800-662-HELP.

For those of you who know someone suffering from addiction, please don't hesitate to speak up, especially on a matter such as this. Time is of the essence, and it's critical that we help someone now.

I wish you all the best.

Rebecca

"The world is full of suffering; it is also full of overcoming it."

– Helen Keller

One • Chloe

I've acted oblivious to my parents growing further apart over the past six months. Dad works long hours on most evenings, coming home well past midnight. Mom and I eat dinner, and then she piles on the couch to watch Lifetime movies, sip her wine, and bawl her eyes out. I used to think she cried because of the sappy stories, but as time passed, I realized she cried because she's losing Dad.

So this will be our last summer at the lake house. At least, that's what I keep telling myself. There won't be additional memories created on the lake, riding in my parents' boat. There won't be late-night bonfires by the water. No more talk of planning the following year's vacation and how we can't wait to come back. More than anything, though, I wish they would've told me about this trip prior to packing our bags and hitting the old, dusty trail because now I'm stuck with two people who can't stand the sight of one another. I'm betting money they plan on releasing the giant elephant in the room upon our return home.

This illusion of a perfect life is all just a show, and I'm the audience.

I pull out one of my ear plugs. Listening to music for the past three hours has bored me to death. "How much farther?" I ask.

"Almost there, Chloe," Mom replies. "We'll make a quick stop at the Grab-N-Go to pick up a few items, so if you need anything while we're there, let us know."

They always buy groceries before heading to the lake house. Mom loads us up with plenty of snacks and sandwich food, while Dad hauls cases of soda and water to the car. Just like the old days when our family was happy.

A few miles later, Dad maneuvers the car into a parking space outside the familiar, mid-sized building. It's lunchtime, and the place is swarming with an assortment of tourists and locals.

"You sure you don't need anything while we're in here?" Mom asks once more. "Last chance."

"Nope. I'm good."

As they exit the car, I step out, too, stretching my legs and inhaling fresh air. Being trapped with a couple of adults who haven't said two words to each other in the last week is pretty awkward. I just wish they'd lay their problems on a table and get this divorce thing over with.

I shudder at the thought of the D word, even though it's inevitable.

Closing my eyes, I draw in a deep breath and release. I will *not* let my parents' problems come between me and an unforgettable summer. I'll attempt to enjoy every minute I have with them because we'll never get a do-over. I can be the daughter they want, and in the meantime, I can act as if they were still in love. After all, they're probably here for my sake.

"Mind opening that for me?" Dad motions with his head toward the back end of the Toyota RAV4. I open the rear door.

Mom's not far behind, lugging grocery bags tight with commodities, which look like they'll bust at any second. I watch my parents in that short amount of time; Dad pretends like he doesn't see Mom's arms weighed down with supplies, and Mom pretends like she doesn't see him notice her.

"Here, I'll take a couple," I say, because the white plastic digs into her skin.

"Thanks, honey."

The expanse of silence between these two is amazing, really. How can people loathe each other so much, yet put on a show for the benefit of their daughter? I know one thing: I can't wait to be alone; away from my parents, away from the real world. I'll go for a jog like I always do once I unpack. There's just something about the openness of this place, something that drives me to spread my non-existent wings and soar through the trees with the warm sun adhering to my forehead, nose, and cheeks. Running has that effect on my soul; it's a form of escape, lifting the stress of the world off my shoulders and placing it elsewhere for the time being. Therapy at its best.

One additional happy memory springs to mind when I reflect on my vacations here:

When I was much younger and less troubled, Mom and Dad agreed I could bring a friend to Sandy Shores. Jessica Huntington. She and I were inseparable in middle school. We did the usual girlie stuff at that age: slumber parties, wear each other's clothes, dream we were dating celebrity crushes, dream we were dating real-life crushes. So when our parents allowed Jessica to spend the summer with us, we were both beyond ecstatic. We could only imagine the adventures that'd take place over the summer: the cute boys we could ogle and drool over, sunbathing, chugging lemonade like it was the last thing we'd ever drink.

On the second night of our stay, Jessica and I slipped out for a walk. Winding through the scraggly brush and wild grass around the lake, we stumbled upon an aged, forsaken cottage. Perfect hideout material. What we were hiding from, exactly, I still don't know. The world, maybe? Because when it was just the two of us, alone, in a frightening house, the world outside didn't exist. We told ghost stories and were terrified every time a breeze rustled branches or leaves, certain it was the Boogeyman. Each night thereafter we waited until lights out before we exited my parents' lake house. Each night the stories grew scarier, the house older, and the wind more blatant in its attempts to alarm us.

It was the best and worst summer of my life.

Toward the end of our vacation, Jessica's mom drove to Sandy Shores to pick her up. No phone call. No warning. I remember my parents having a brief discussion with Jessica's mom in the driveway, their faces swallowed in grief, as I stood at the front door. I was too young at the time to understand why Jessica had to leave. What did we do wrong? Did my parents know about our late-night outings? Had I offended them somehow?

It wasn't until we returned home that my parents explained the totality of the situation: Jessica's dad was in a car accident, and he didn't survive. I was heartbroken for her. She missed school for two weeks, and when she returned, things changed. *She* changed. It was almost as if she was embarrassed that I was around to witness her dad's passing. Or maybe every time she saw me, I was the poster child for the horrible incident.

We never spoke of what happened that night. Actually, we never really spoke again. Jessica moved on to a more popular crowd, became a cheerleader freshman year, and began dating a football player—typical high school clichés. As for me, I stuck with track, buried my nose in books, and kept to myself. But every now and again, I caught Jessica glancing my way. Nothing that garnered attention from her new clique, but it was enough to chip off a piece of my heart.

So now, when I look at my dad, at how he's abandoning Mom and me for a younger, livelier girl who we've never met, I think about Jessica's dad, about how he never had a choice when parting from his family. My dad has willingly made that decision, and part of me hates him for it.

I refocus as we reach our driveway. Small pebbles crunch under the tires like a long procession of bubble wrap, and the scent of freshly-mowed grass invades the vents. Not the most glamorous smell in the world, but it definitely reminds me of summertime.

Our lake house hasn't changed once in the years I've visited. The paint job impersonates a pale sun, and the white shutters remind me of clean linen. Inside, seashells and starfish adorn the walls, which are painted the same pastel yellow as the outside. Trust me, if I've told my mom once, I've told her a hundred times: we don't live on the beach, so the decorations need to go. A lakeside beach, maybe. But a real beach? Nada. And every single time she replies, "Seashells and starfish remind people of beaches, and beaches remind people of vacation, which is what we're on, is it not?"

"Help me get these drinks in the fridge, will ya, pumpkin?" Dad says as we lug groceries in. Setting the drinks on the kitchen counter, he separates plastic rings from the sodas, and I grab the newly-freed cans to place in the refrigerator.

Mom carries the last of the grocery bags and begins

emptying their contents. "Looks like we have plenty of food for the next two weeks," she says. "I'll have to make another trip after that."

Dad smiles weakly; it would've been imperceptible if I hadn't been paying attention. He and I finish stockpiling the drinks, and he disappears from the kitchen. My guess is he's searching for a reason to hide from Mom.

She notices his absence, too.

"Well," she blurts, but it comes out as more of a huff than a word.

"I'm sure he's just ready to unpack like the rest of us," I lie. "It's been a long day."

Pausing midway to the cabinets, she says, "It's been a long year," so quietly that I want to tap my eardrums to ensure they're still receptive. But the moment passes, and she finishes storing the goodies. "Listen, honey, why don't you follow your father's lead and unpack your things? You'll feel better once you get situated."

Don't push me away, Mom. I'm all you've got.

"Sure," I say with a smile, abstaining from my subconscious words.

Upstairs, I bypass my parents' room. The door is closed, except for a two-inch gap, and Dad speaks so quietly his voice is ghostlike. I back up, peeking through the crack. He paces back and forth across a four-foot space at the end of the bed, combing his fingers through his hair a bit too gruffly. He seems bewildered.

"Can't this wait?" he hisses into his cell phone. "Jesus Christ, Oksana, I'm on vacation with my family . . . No, of course not . . . You *know* I want to; I just can't escape right now."

My body abruptly jerks back as if an unseen force pushes me. Escape? Nobody's holding you prisoner, Dad. Last I checked, Mom and I aren't guards, and our home isn't Alcatraz. I lean closer to the door when his voice becomes more restrained.

"Fine. You know what? I'll see what I can do . . . Yeah, give me a couple of days to figure something out . . . I'll call you, all right? . . . I miss you, too. Bye."

Crap! I pad lightly down the hall to my bedroom. His door swings open just as mine closes. Releasing a long, dejected sigh, I will my legs to move toward the bed, where I collapse, burying my face in my pillow.

Several minutes tick by before I pull myself together. After all, I kind of saw this coming, didn't I? I mean, it's obvious he's had someone else. So, why is it tough to hear him actually speaking to her? Maybe it's the fact that he's abandoning *our* family vacation for some cheap skank he probably met at an office party. Maybe it's the fact that he's leading us on, not just Mom, but me. Or maybe it's the fact that our summer house evokes loud memories of a time not so long ago, when a father was in love with his family, and a daughter was in love with her life.

Why can't he just file the divorce papers and liberate

himself?

Ugh. Screw this. I unzip my luggage case, finding exactly what I need—gym clothes. Settling on a pair of yoga pants and a tank top, I snatch my iPod and sneakers, and head downstairs. Dad's nowhere to be found, and Mom's staring out at the tranquil abyss of the lake water.

"I'm going for a run. Be back later," I tell her as I slide open the glass doors leading to the rear deck.

"Okay, honey," she murmurs, too absorbed in whatever weighs on her mind to notice I'm leaving, to even *look* at me.

I shake my head. This summer is going to be dandy.

Cranking up the volume on my iPod, I scroll through the list of albums, settling on *30 Seconds to Mars*. Rock has the perfect effect on me when running. All my anger, all my aggression just . . . vanishes. I can free my mind in the warm, humid air with the help of music.

On this occasion, I take an alternative route. Sometimes change is good; it challenges the spirit. Dodging overgrowth and sticks, I sample my surroundings. All is quiet on the lake so far. By this time next week, everyone will be on the water. I wish we'd take the boat out one last time, but clearly my dad will bail on us at the first opportune moment for his sleaze of the week.

I shake my head to dispel the idea of him being so hurtful. How can he treat us like this and get away with it?

My feet stop before my brain fully registers why. Looming in front of me is the abandoned cottage Jessica and I frequented as kids. I can't believe someone hasn't bulldozed the place after all these years. Tentatively, I take careful steps forward. *It's not like the place will collapse due to your arrival, Chloe.* The house is exactly how I remember it: chipped paint, missing shingles, shattered windows. It's as if I'm stuck in a time warp. Like, I'll turn around and Jessica won't be far behind.

My hand pushes the front door open, and the hinges groan under exertion. I wipe my fingers, now coated in a thick layer of dirt, on my pants. Surveying the property, the first thing I notice are the missing floorboards. I make a mental note to watch where I step. The furniture from a different era sits sheathed under once-white sheets, which have now darkened to a rich russet. In the corner is a skinny, three-legged, round-top table, most likely used at one point to hold a vase filled with brightly-colored flowers. But that might be my imagination talking.

Finding an area in the middle of the living room floor, I tap my foot on the wooden beams to test my weight. They don't budge. *Good.* Sitting down, I close my eyes, imagining Jessica and I are back in our perfect little world, in our perfect little cottage. Moonlight was the only form of brightness so we could see. Her lips would curve into a wicked grin, one that meant she was ready for another fearsome night. She'd begin dishing out her imaginative tale about a man who obsessed over dead children, about killing them and eating them for breakfast—way too morbid for our age, which made the account that much scarier. And when she'd land on a terrifying element of her story, she'd flick on the flashlight, illuminating her face in a bright but creepy beam. I'd squeal, even though I knew it was coming, eventually; I just didn't know when.

"And they never knew what became of him," she'd always say at the end of her stories.

I smile to myself. "What *did* become of him, Jessica?" I ask in the here and now. Opening my eyes, I shriek. A boy, not much older than me, stands a few feet away. His short brown hair is disheveled, and his jade eyes cut into mine.

The corner of his mouth twitches. "Who's Jessica?"

Two • Chloe

Scrambling upright, the floorboards protest under my weight. "I-I'm sorry. I didn't know anyone lived here. I was just . . ." My voice trails off. "Wait—*do* you live here?"

He bypasses me without a response, drops his belongings in the corner of the room, and then directs his attention at me. "Not permanently, I don't. Who the hell would? I mean, look at this place." He points toward the crumbling ceiling with both index fingers in an obvious attempt to tell me, *Yes, you have lost your mind.*

"Oh."

"I'm a squatter," he offers. "I move from place to place

whenever I feel like it."

Hmm. This is strange, and awkward. "So, are you from around here?"

A short laugh spouts past his lips. "Oh, no, no, no. I don't do the personal shit."

"Well, you could at least tell me if I need to call someone for you. A family member, maybe? A friend?" I cross my arms over my chest. "You can't stay here. This place could drop at any minute; it's not safe."

He chuckles and raises one eyebrow. God, he has a pretty smile. "And you give a damn because . . .?"

Okay, I lied. His smile isn't that pretty. "Um, I give a damn because I have a heart and care about humanity, which is more than I can say for you, apparently."

He raises his hands in mock surrender. "You've got me. You know exactly how I feel about the whole of society. Now, can you go? I have . . . needs to take care of and you're only making me itch."

I purse my lips. *Don't do it, Chloe! Don't say it!* "You're a jackass." The words are out before I can stop myself from saying them. Turning on my heel, I storm through the front door and out to the lawn. I can't believe the nerve of this guy! He doesn't even reside in that house, yet he more or less kicked me out. I should call the cops, but something about the way he said he has needs just unravels me.

A little snooping won't hurt, will it? Ducking low, I

noiselessly trek to one of the windows at the back of the house. Okay, this may not be the best idea I've ever had, and I probably won't make a great private investigator, *ever*, but what the hell.

A couple of windows down from where he placed his belongings is where I want to be. That way, if he catches me, I can run. So far, though, I can't see anything; the glass is too cluttered with grime. I move down to another window. This one has better visibility than the last and—*oh, my God!* The answer smacks me across my face as a sharp breath rakes over the tips of my teeth. For a moment, I stand mesmerized by the way he ties off his arm and lights up a spoon, then fills a syringe and injects himself. His head falls back in bittersweet suffering, eyes closed, as he lets the needle drop to the filthy floor. I feel like I'm having an out-of-body experience as I watch him. He's so . . . so . . . *free*. Relaxed. I know that feeling; I'm that way with running. It's a distraction, a way to unshackle my mind.

Taking a careful step back, I realize I can't stand here and watch him forever, even though I want nothing more than to run inside, throw my arms around his neck, and tell him everything's going to be all right. Although this is a serious wake-up call by the universe, I have to get home. I sincerely hope Mom's still not standing at the kitchen doors when I return. I've seen that look on her face before; it's followed by Lifetime movies, potato chips, and a bottle of cheap wine. Which, I hate to say it, may be a good thing for tonight, because I plan on cooking up a little something-something myself . . . and it's not drugs.

14

I bound back the way I came, back to the summer house. Inside, my suspicions are more or less confirmed when I see Mom curled up on the couch, under a throw, flipping through TV channels.

She glances toward me. "Hey, baby. How was your run?"

"Good, Mom." Well, as good as it can be when one finds a drug addict living in a deserted house. I study the kitchen and living room, and realize Dad's not here. *Of course.* "Where's Dad?" I hate to ask. God, I really, really do. It's not so much the fact that I care where he's at, it's that I *know* he's sneaking around. And, quite frankly, I'm certain Mom knows, too.

"He, uh . . ." She clears her throat. "His friend Dan called and wanted to meet up for a beer or two. He'll be home later." She smiles sweetly, but the full effect doesn't reach her eyes.

Oh, she knows.

"You going to watch a movie?" I ask.

Without looking at me, she replies, "I haven't decided yet. There's nothing on, really." And then she turns, facing my way. "Why? Is there something in particular you'd like to see?"

I shake my head. "No, I think I'm going to take a shower and rest. I'm drained from the drive." Her emotions wane a bit, so I quickly add, "Rain check for tomorrow?"

"Sure, baby," she murmurs, twisting to face the TV again.

Whew! That was close. I dash upstairs to my bedroom, dig through my luggage case for some clean clothes, and sprint to the shower. Soaking under hot water and letting my mind melt together with the heat, I concoct a plan. Towel-drying myself, I slip on some sweat pants and a T-shirt, and glare at myself in the mirror.

"You can do this, Chloe," I say, narrowing my eyes at my reflection. "Don't be a pussy. Don't back down."

There. Done. Nothing like a little self-motivation to get the ball rolling.

In a little bit, when the effects of my mom's wine have taken hold, and when the drug has run its course in that poor, strange boy, I'm going to take him some food. He can stand to gain a few pounds. Not that he's bone-thin, but still. Whatever happens when I confront him, I'm going to hold my own. He needs some serious help, and I can't be this innocent bystander who does nothing about it. That's like watching a kid being bullied, and pretending I don't see the taunts and jabs happen. More than that, if I turn my back on him now, I'll always be faced with what-ifs: *What if* I didn't help him and his life turns tragic? *What if* there was a sliver of possibility I could turn him in the right direction? *What if* I could at least say I tried, even though he discarded my reasons?

You're doing the right thing, I tell myself. I mean, what if nobody's bothered to help him? Worse, what if he doesn't have anybody *to* help him? No parents, no friends, no nothing. The thought leaves a bitter taste in my mouth. I steady my breath and concentrate on my mantra: *You can do this. You can do this. You can do this.*

16

Obviously, he's very stubborn. And irritating. And ridiculous. Who sleeps in a ramshackle home, anyway?

Someone who doesn't have a home, my intuition chimes in. Yes, of course. But what about homeless shelters, other places to seek refuge? I shake my head. I know nothing of that lifestyle. I can at least say I tried, even if he refuses my little peace offering for calling him a jackass earlier. But what if he chose this life? What if he *wants* to be homeless and drug-addicted? Surely not. Surely my mind is being a Negative Nancy.

I head downstairs to the kitchen, rifling through the cabinets to see what all Mom bought. This boy needs *real* food, sustenance. Nourishment for his wrecked body. Okay, we have bread, but do we have sandwich meat? Opening the fridge, I search the lower drawers and—*yes, we do!* Cha-ching! I feel like I've won the lottery, although I'm not entirely certain why I'm so excited about this. I have the distinct feeling I'll be rejected.

Grabbing a jar of mayo, I spread it on both sides of the bread, followed by lettuce, tomato, cheese, and turkey. Mom bought some Nacho Cheese Doritos at the store—*yum!*—so I cram them into one Ziploc bag and shove the sandwich in another. I scan the inside of the refrigerator, settling on bottled water and snatching one for the road. Glancing over my shoulder to see what Mom's doing, I realize she's in a daze while watching one of her fictional TV shows. Can't say I didn't see that one coming.

"I'll be back in a bit, Mom!" I call as I rush out the back

door.

My stomach's knotted up so tightly I'm certain a Boy Scout would have a field day trying to untie it. I deepen my breaths, inhaling and exhaling in a slow, rhythmic pattern. *Don't chicken out!* Yeah, yeah. That's the last thing I want to do. In my very limited experience with loners, they tend to either like being isolated or secretly want somebody to notice them. Maybe this neglected guy just needs some reassurance.

Creeping along the backside of the cottage, I peer through the same window as earlier . . . and he's nowhere to be seen. Where the hell did he go? One look around the vicinity and inside the house tells me he's left. Now, more relaxed, I traipse through the dense grass to the front door. The house is as empty and quiet as it was when I arrived earlier, before he showed up.

But his belongings are still piled in the corner.

Placing the sandwich, Doritos, and bottled water by his backpack, I turn to leave. Sunlight glimmers off the metal tip of the syringe lying on the floor, and I'm fascinated. What does this toothpick-sized object give him? Ecstasy? Momentary rapture from real life? If there's one thing I've learned during my high school years it's that one doesn't touch a needle—HIV and all that—but now that I'm face to face with the gadget, I can't look away; it's like telling a child not to grab for candy in a candy store.

Okay, I won't *really* come in contact with it, but I am critically questioning my self-control at the moment.

"What the fuck are you doing?"

I whirl around, nearly tripping on my own feet. There, in all his glory, is the boy . . . and he's soaking wet, T-shirt removed.

"Oh, I'm sorry." He doesn't look convinced of my apology. "I-I brought you something to eat. I thought you might be hungry."

He breezes past, heading toward his property. After one glance, he pivots to confront me. "Did you touch my shit?" His eyes are a fierce green, the color magnified only by his intense expression.

I shake my head. "Uh, no." One of his eyebrows rises in disbelief. "Honestly, I didn't. I looked, but didn't touch."

Pursing his lips, he says low and slow, "Don't go near my things, and don't come near me again. I'm warning you."

A feathery tickle brushes up my spine. Who the hell does he think he is, threatening me? My little pep talk with the mirror thirty minutes ago is still fresh on my mind. "First of all, don't talk to me like that. Second, I'll touch whoever's shit I want to. You're not the boss of me." *Way to go, Chloe. You've officially won first place in the I-sound-like-a-sixth-grader competition.*

Surprisingly, he smirks. "Is that a fact?"

"It's a fact."

We glare at each other for what seems like a matter of minutes, but in reality, I'm sure it's less than ten seconds.

"You should go," he says finally, breaking the glacial ice that has wedged its way between us.

19

I huff. "And leave you here? Not gonna happen."

The quizzical look on his face speaks volumes.

I continue, "You need help, and I'm here to offer you mine."

I expect a rampage, a riot, something of that sort, but all I receive is laughter, dark and intimidating, echoing from deep inside. Eventually, the laughter dies down, as does his comical expression.

"Get lost, bitch," he states flatly.

Oh. Hell. No. Because my adrenaline has spiked, and because he's pissing me off, I do the only logical thing my brain can process: I walk straight up to him and punch his face. Reeling back, I shake away the surge of pain tingling through my hand and wrist.

"Ow!" He retreats, rubbing his cheek. "What the hell was that for?"

"Because you need some sense knocked into you. Now, I'll say this again: I'm not leaving until you eat, and I'm not leaving until you accept some form of assistance, whether it's from me or otherwise." *Good, Chloe. Remember: don't just stand aside and watch this main event unfold.*

"Fuck this," he says, packing what little items he owns and shouldering his backpack. On his way out, he stops by my side, shoulder to shoulder, so close I can feel his breath on my cheek. "You know, it's people like you who made me this way."

And with that, ladies and gentlemen, the hellion exits the building.

Three • Logan

Help me? When has anybody ever helped me? The one and only time my parents offered to do anything remotely close, they were ready to shell out thousands of dollars for *other* people to recommend what I should and shouldn't be doing with my life. Not them. Not my so-called family. And my friends? To hell with them. They're long gone by now.

Well, you could at least tell me if I need to call someone for you. Even if I took the bitch up on her offer, who will she call when it's all said and done, when I've sobered up?

You need help. Her words reverberate through my head. God, why can't it be that easy? Why can't I turn myself in and let somebody show me the light, or whatever it's called. I mean, yeah, obviously it'd be nice for a change.

I shake my head.

No, it wouldn't. I've chosen this. I've set my destiny in motion. One day, I'll die because of this obsessive love for all things bad, and my parents will be void of one less child. Then I think of Lucas, my younger bro. What does he think about me leaving? What have Mom and Dad told him? I never said goodbye to the little man. I'm supposed to be some kind of an example—aren't all big brothers?—but that idea flew out the fucking window a long, long time ago when they kicked me out of my own home.

Gahh. Frustrating sons of bi—

"Where are you going?"

I glance over my shoulder. Great. She's following me now. I officially have a stalker.

Ignoring her, I press on. What's with this girl, anyway? I can't count on my fingers and toes the number of times people have passed me in the street without offering their help, so why her? Why now?

Although, she is pretty hot; I will give her that. I've always had a thing for blondes, especially ones with big, blue eyes, but she's a-whole-nother level, one that's out of my league. Besides, I meant what I said about people like her getting me into this mess. If I had never joined the football team with those rich, preppy fuckers, I'm positive everything would be different. Fate, however, had a different plan for me.

"So, you're just going to ignore me and wander off without a shirt?"

I snort. *Yes and yes. Can I be any more obvious? Take a damn hint.*

"You know," she says, "I'm just going to follow you until you give in."

Okay, that does it. I wheel around. "Dude, what's it going to take for you to leave me alone? You're not going to follow me, and I'm not going to listen to you. I don't need your help or anyone else's. Don't you think I would've been treated by now if I really wanted the extra hand? Don't you *get* it?"

Her eyes widen, then return to their usual arrogant glower. "Fine." She shrugs. "Have it your way. When you realize how badly you need my help, I'll be waiting in the lake house down from the cottage. You can't miss it; it's pastel yellow with white shutters."

Shaking my head, I say, "Won't happen." Turning my back on her and walking away, I shout, "Run home to Mommy and Daddy," and chuck deuces in the air.

I head in the general direction of town; there's an alley somewhere out there, calling my name. I'll hang around the area until dusk, and then find a place to sleep. I find myself reminiscing about the first night I snoozed on concrete, lodged between the day's leftovers and other shit I don't even want to remember, outside Bernie's Bar & Grille. I was so damn hungry I had to force the bile down my throat long enough to scrounge through the dumpsters for a semi-eaten meal. It was utterly disgusting. Probably the grossest thing I've done in my life.

But that's become the norm for me. How else would I still be alive? All the money I had saved was withdrawn from the bank the day my parents pushed me out of our home, and the cash was used to buy what I was already addicted to—heroin. Now I have to stay away from Big P and his boys. I owe them a serious sum of funds. Funds I don't have. I've led them on for this long, but I don't know how much more this can continue. If they find out about my family . . .

I shake away the thought. Every move I've made has prevented them from learning about Mom, Dad, and Lucas.

I often wonder if I'll ever run into my parents in Sandy Shores. They live in the next town over, but surely they've figured out by now that I'm not remote. I mean, I guess I could've hitched a ride to a city far from here, but what good would that have done? Can they still feel me in their hearts, or have they given up on me completely?

Stopping by the side of the road, I drag a shirt out of my backpack and pull it over my head. Cars coast by, lazily, like they have all the time in the world. Once there's a break, I cross the main street. Up ahead, Jake strums his guitar and croons a song he wrote, while tourists empty the contents of their wallets into his case. If I had a natural talent like his, I'd be set for life.

"'Sup, Jake?" I say in passing.

He nods once, his dreads swaying a little, but continues singing the melody. He and I have known each other for a few months now. His family split in different directions, and he chose songwriting and performing over an alternative lifestyle, never looking back. I wish I had the ability to do the same, but every day I'm haunted by images of a life that might still exist for me if I choose to go a dissimilar route.

This time of day, everyone is either eating dinner or concluding shopping on the strip. Although it'll never happen, I silently implore that, at some point, my parents and Lucas will stroll up one of the sidewalks and we'll bump into each other. Lucas will throw his tiny arms around my neck as I squeeze him in a hug. Mom and Dad will apologize, and then invite me home. We'll pretend none of this ever happened.

But that's just it—pretend. Make believe. My mind working overtime.

Still, I scan both sides of the street.

I can always tell the difference between tourists and locals. Tourists frequent the T-shirt shops more than anyone, searching for the perfect souvenir, the perfect reminder of their vacation. A trinket to set on a shelf to collect dust until the next year. Locals unwind, enjoying the sun and food.

I slide into a chair on the deck at Bernie's, setting my backpack into the seat beside me. A waitress wastes no time pausing by my table, asking what I'd like to drink.

"Water," I tell her.

She eyes me up and down, like a pest who doesn't belong. I sympathize with her, because in a way, I don't belong anywhere.

"Will that be all?" she asks, pen at the ready above her notepad.

"Yeah, that's all."

"You're not going to eat?" Now she's wound up.

Later, when I rummage through your garbage bins. "Nope."

She rolls her eyes and sashays inside. Returning with my drink, she practically drops the cup on the table, water sloshing over the rim. I jerk back. She cocks one eyebrow, daring me to say something, but I give up, deflated, and she moves on to another table.

I hadn't realized how thirsty I was until I take the first swig. Between injecting myself and going for a quick swim, apparently my mouth dried out. My stomach growls, too, but I'll deal with that later. Right now, I want to sip my water, chill, and question the motives for that annoying girl at the lake. Does she think I'm a charity case? Or was she just throwing a pity party? Either way, there's something different about her. Something I haven't faced in a long time. Given the right circumstances, and the right mindset, I might've agreed to her offer. As it stands, though, she's too damn proud to win me over. I rub my cheek, wondering if it's red from her hit. She has an arm, but nothing I can't handle.

My thoughts are jolted back to reality when, behind me, there's commotion. Women cry out, shuffling their children out of the way. Husbands guard their wives. What the hell? I squint, as if that will actually give me heightened, catlike senses to see what's going on. As the crowd moves aside, my heart thrums five times faster. *No.* Big P and his boys are heckling Jake, their voices carrying to the outdoor patio where I sit.

"Where is he, man? I know you know," Big P taunts.

Jake shrugs and shakes his head. "I don't know, man. Haven't seen him around here in a while." He strums three chords on his guitar, as if that will make Big P get the hell out of dodge.

Oh, shit. I shoulder my backpack and prep myself to run when Big P snatches the guitar out of Jake's hands and smashes it against the concrete, wood splintering into several pieces.

"Hey, hey, hey!" Jake yells, standing up. "What's your problem, bro?"

"My problem," says Big P, "is that you know where he is and you're covering his damn tracks. Now, tell me where I can find him before your face is the next thing to collide against the street."

"Look, man, if I knew, I'd tell you." There's a nervous tinge to Jake's voice.

No, no, no, Jake. Don't let them hear that.

Too late.

Two of Big P's boys—B and Ice—fist the back of Jake's shirt, picking him up midair, and slamming him to the ground. His face meets the concrete with a loud *crack.* Damn it. They pick him up again, his nose spouting blood, and prepare to do the

27

stunt all over again.

"Last chance," says Big P. "Where is he?"

Jake can't even utter words; he's probably in shock, and pain.

B and Ice get the nod of approval from Big P, but before they do some serious damage to his face, I shout, "Hey, assholes! Over here!"

That gets their attention. They drop Jake and gradually stalk my way. By now, everyone on both sides of the road watch in anticipation of what'll happen next. I'm surprised nobody's called the cops. God, that's the last thing I need.

"Get him!"

B and Ice sprint toward me, and I bolt over the low patio railing and up the road, taking a detour through one of the alleys. Of course there's a fence at the end. I launch myself halfway up the chain links, hauling my body over the frame, and land on two feet. B and Ice have caught up, though. I pump my legs into a sprint, bounding out the back of the lane, through the rear parking lot, and over small hills of grass and wildflowers.

"You can't hide from us!" one of them yells from behind me. I think it's Ice, or maybe it's B. Either way, my brain is too busy at the moment to give a damn which.

I'm too out of shape. If this had happened back in the day, back when I was still lifting weights and throwing footballs across the field, I would've outrun these guys by now. But here I am, racing from two men who are pretty much the equivalent of bodyguards. Two men who probably have guns.

Ahead, two of the main streets intersect. *Get past the crossroads.* Cars are everywhere; waiting on the light to change, waiting to make a turn, waiting, waiting, waiting. I don't have time to wait. I bolt through the traffic, vehicles slamming on their brakes, nearly missing me. That's okay, because the alternative would be getting taken out by Ice and B, maybe even tortured until Big P decides how he wants to use his new toys on my skin. Carving. Slicing. Chopping. Nothing new for him; the man gets what he wants, when he wants it.

Momentarily, I'm sidetracked by the flash of blue lights and the wail of a siren. *NO! Not now.* I don't stop, though. Every strand in me is pushing my body, my mind, *me*, to stay alive. I'll get their money. I will.

"Son!" A car door slams shut behind me, and I risk a glance over my shoulder. The cop is now pursuing me on foot. "Slow down! Get back here!"

I recognize him. It's Charles, one of my dad's friends.

Before slowing to a complete stop, I double check the area beyond Charles's car. B and Ice are nowhere to be seen. I'm sure they saw the police logo and decided to bail.

"What the hell are you doing out here? Who are you running from?" Charles, like me, bends over at the waist to catch his breath. He hasn't been in the best of shape since his stroke a couple of years back. I should've known better than to push him.

"You didn't see them? They . . . I . . ."

Charles straightens up. "Who?"

I shake my head, leveling myself, too. I have to lean against a tree, though; I'm too dizzy. "Nothing. Never mind. Just some crazy kids."

He gives me this look that says he knows I'm lying, but he doesn't push the subject. "You know . . . Ah, God . . ." He peers up at the clear sky, as if that'll help him find his words. "Your mom and dad have been worried about you."

I don't want to talk about them right now. Jesus, Charles, give it a break. I try opening my mouth to speak, but my throat feels like it's clogged with cotton balls.

"Your mom went out looking for ya after that night," he carries on. "She was so distraught. Your dad, too. He hasn't been taking this so well."

"And Lucas?" I murmur hoarsely.

Charles purses his mouth, hands grasping his hips. "About as good as a twelve-year-old kid can be. They've kept him busy with sports and all, hoping it'll keep his mind off the way things are."

I nod. "Good. It's better that way."

"Better for whom? Them, or you? 'Cause the way I see it, none of you picked a particularly great way to show your admiration for one another." He pauses, maybe reflecting on that night, maybe reflecting on the effect it's had on my parents and Lucas since. "They shouldn't have done that to ya, Logan. It was wrong."

"Yeah, well, they did." *Can we* please *not talk about this?* "Can't undo the past. What's done is done."

"No, but you can learn from the past, even if it isn't your friend."

I snort. "There's no going back. They've made their decision pretty clear: they don't want me around."

"For God's sake, boy! Are you listening to yourself? They kicked you out for a reason." He seizes the moment to collect himself. "Look, your father never gave me all the details of why they did what they did, but he reassured me it was for your own good. Now, I'm not sayin' I agree with them one hundred percent, but I think there's more to it. I think if you collected yourself and agreed to work things out, they'd welcome you back with open arms. But, as it stands, you're up Shit Creek."

I roll my eyes, letting my backpack fall from my shoulder. *He didn't tell you because you're a cop.* "Nothing will ever be the same again, because they'll never trust me."

"What was it, Logan? Theft? Underage drinking? Drugs?" he asks.

I almost lose my composure at the last mention. "Don't worry about it, Charles. You go on doing your thing, and I'll do mine."

He sighs. "Well, whatever it was, it had to be pretty bad. I've never known of your parents to be so upset about something."

Bad. Bad. Bad. You're a bad person.

"It was," is all I say, managing to swallow past the lump in

31

my throat. The aching dryness has returned, and I suddenly wish I had my water.

"Well, uh, do you need a ride somewhere? Is there someplace you're staying?" He wipes the back of his neck.

He's just prying, probably so he can give my parents answers. Answers I don't really want them to have right now. "I live all over, moving from here to there when I feel like it. It's not terrible." *Liar.*

"So, can I give ya a ride?" His eyes implore mine for a sign, something he can latch onto, to keep his conscience satisfied.

In response, I barely move my head. *No, Charles. Just . . . no.*

His eyes leave mine as he nods. "Well, don't get into any trouble. I don't want to be the one to bring ya in."

"I'll try," I mumble.

"Take care of yourself, Logan," he says as he turns and walks back to his car.

"Bye, Charles," I breathe, battling my subconscious mind. *Go after him! Go home!* But I meant what I said about it not being that easy. My parents would've found me by now if they wanted to work things out, wouldn't they? And it's their fault I'm in this situation to begin with; it was their idea for me to be a 'team player,' as Dad called it. They put too much pressure on me to be the perfect quarterback, the superstar god of the football field. They could've at least acted like responsible adults instead of pushing me.

They were always pushing me.

At school. *"C's in three of your classes? Logan, how will you ever get a football scholarship with grades like these?"*

On the field. *"You get your ass out there and score a touchdown! I don't care if you dislocate your arm in the process; you do what you gotta do."*

Out the front door. *"We can't do it anymore, Logan. We just can't let you stay here. Lucas can't ever look up to someone like you, and your mom and I, well, we don't really know what happened to our son or what you've done with him, but you're not the boy we raised."*

Pushing me away, away, away.

Four • Chloe

So he won't go down without a fight. That's fine. I can live with that. I've watched *Intervention* enough to know when a drug addict goes through the five stages, and he's definitely piggy-back riding Addiction—maybe even Denial. Or is that only for alcoholics?

I wander back to the lake house, taking my sweet time. Mom will wonder where I've been, why earlier I darted out so quickly. *More fresh air, Mom, because the air between you and Dad is too congested for my breathing.*

Several teenagers sail down the lake in a boat, wildly squealing with laughter as they tease one another. *That should be me*. I should be having the time of my life every single summer I visit Sandy Shores. I should be creating memories with friends, or be showing off for that one boy who stole my heart. Instead, I'm standing here, on the shore, watching my would-be life pass by.

My eyes never leave the boat until they've completely disappeared from sight. Where they're headed, I don't know. Anywhere is better than here.

Mom mutes the TV when I enter through the kitchen. "Where were you?" she asks.

I open the cabinets, searching for a distraction, and a cup. "Out." It's always like this between us. She's so patronizing and nosey when it comes to my personal life that I can't help but throw up a brick wall. And if I tell her about trying to help a drug addict, well, she'd blow a gasket.

"That's not what I asked you," she pushes.

I don't respond, which is my usual choice comeback. Grabbing a glass, I move toward the refrigerator, which is—thankfully—out of Mom's line of sight. As I close the door, I jump at her sudden appearance in the entryway, her arms crossed, searching for a fight. I know how this ends.

Ignoring her, I fill my cup with ice and soda, then take a sip without looking her in the eyes.

"Chloe," she warns, "I'm not going to ask you again."

"Then don't," I say, shrugging. "I don't see what the big deal is, anyway. We're supposed to have these awesome summers here, yet you guys still keep an invisible collar on me at all times. I'm not a toddler, Mom—"

"I never said you were."

"—so don't treat me like one."

She squeezes her eyes shut, like she's in some insurmountable amount of pain that nobody but her feels. "When you are in my house, you have to abide by my rules."

See, normally I'd say something along the lines of "Okay, Mom" and stalk up to my bedroom. But this year is different. Since she and Dad dragged me into their relationship woes, I don't care about making them happy, making them believe we're this perfect family. So, why pretend?

In the obedient response's place, Mom gets: "Yeah, but it's not your house; it's Dad's. And he's not exactly here right now, is he?" God, that hurt me more than it hurt her, I think, but all this hatred I've harbored for the past six months has swollen inside my mind and body, petitioning me to release it.

Wish granted.

Mom bites her lip and opens her eyes, nodding. Without saying another word, she glides back to the couch, covers up under a throw, and un-mutes the TV.

I sigh. I don't want things to be like this between us. I want to be there for her, but every time I've tried starting a conversation about her and Dad's problems, she'd change the subject, basically telling me it's none of my business. Well—*news flash!*—it is my business. I'm *their* daughter. I was created by these two people who were once in love, so I have as much right to know as they do.

But I don't believe for a second either one of them is mature enough to man-up to what's happening. They both realize what's going on behind closed doors, and neither of them says or does anything. They just choose to keep their mouths shut, pretending this isn't a farce. Pretend, pretend, pretend. God, one would think I was born into a family of actors. If that were true, Mom and Dad would've definitely won an Oscar for best duo performance by now.

This summer is turning out worse than I imagined. I had these romantic ideas of Mom and Dad making up while they're away from the boring hum-drum of work and everyday life, but now those notions have flown out the window and latched on to the tip of a breeze, carried off to another state. Maybe even another planet.

I flop onto my bed, staring up at the ceiling. What the hell am I going to do for fun around here? I need something to keep me occupied. And, no offense, but spending all summer watching movies and reality TV shows with my mom is not what I had in mind.

W.W.J.D.

What Would Jessica Do?

If she were here, if her father had never died, what would she and I be doing? Painting our toenails? Gossiping about cute boys, or, dare I even say it, our boyfriends? She doesn't need any help in that department, but it was obvious to everyone at Clear Lakes High School that I did, seeing as I've never actually had one. Unless I count the time Jeremy Frazier and I made out behind the school and he told me I was the most beautiful girl in the world, only to show up to homecoming two weeks later with Melanie what's-her-face. Seriously, I don't even remember her last name. Ugh. *Men.*

The reality of the Jessica situation is that I truly don't know if we'd still be friends, even if that summer never happened. Her destiny always lay with cheerleading and becoming an element of the popular crowd. And mine? Well, I'm not sure what my destiny is, but it probably isn't *this*. I snatch a pillow, cover my face, and scream. Not one of those horror movie, blood-curdling screams—those are obnoxious—but one that feels good. Just to release all my pent-up frustrations aimed at the world.

As I come down from the high, I sheepishly grin to myself . . . and hear a *plat* at my window. Sitting up, I wait; wait to see if it's the stupid birds tapping on the glass or the gutter, wait to make sure my ears aren't hearing things, wait for my heart to lessen its frenzied beating.

Plat.

My body jerks in response. Okay, so I'm not making this up. Slowly, I stand and peep around the edge of the window. Standing in the backyard, looking warily around, is that crazy boy. So he changed his mind, huh? That's . . .

Interesting.

Good, I suppose.

I flip the latch and raise the pane. "Came to your senses, I see."

He glares at me. "I'm not doing this for you."

I shrug. "Of course you aren't; you're doing it for you. At least, that's the goal."

"Look, we need to get some things straight before I agree. Can you come down?"

I smile. "Be right out."

Passing by Mom in the living room, she doesn't even bother to turn around and look at me. There's no telling how long she'll be pissed about our little tiff. Mental note to self: watch a movie with her sometime this week, even if it's torturous.

Outside, the boy waits expectantly, then motions with a backward nod away from the house.

"I figured your parents would ask questions if they saw me," he says as we meander down the lake's shore. "I also figured you were pretty spoiled, so you'd have the best view of the lake."

I roll my eyes and snort. "The whole parents thing? Not likely. My dad's either screwing his tramp girlfriend or tossing back a few beers, and Mom's acting like a chronic-depression sufferer who ran out of meds. And good guess on where my room is, by the way. It would've sucked if it were my parents' bedroom instead."

"Yeah, no shit." He stares at the ground before him, eyebrows creasing in deep thought.

Time to change the subject before this topic becomes a mess. "Earlier, you didn't need my help, so what made you come back?"

He smirks, but the full effect doesn't appear on the rest of his face. "Long story, but the gist is that I'd like to see my little brother again."

"Does he live here?"

"Nearby."

I cross my arms. "Well, that's a good starting point."

He looks at me, then, like he can see straight through to my soul. "Why are you doing this for me? I mean, what's it to you?"

I should ask myself this question a hundred times over before ever agreeing to anything, but the truth of the matter is I feel sorry for the guy. If it were me, if I were down on my luck and holing up in dingy, abandoned houses, I'd be grateful for somebody's help. Grateful, but leery.

"I just wanted something to look forward to this summer," I say, laughing nervously. "Tag. You're it, I guess."

He observes me. "So, how does this work, anyway?"

"Not really sure, but we can, maybe, take it a day at a time?" Crap. That sounds like I'm asking for his approval, which is the exact opposite of what I should be doing for someone in this situation. He needs somebody who will guide him in the right direction, somebody who has soft-yet-firm principles on how to manage his lifestyle. Somebody who knows what the hell they're doing.

"You have no idea," he states flatly.

"I have a *general* idea. That doesn't mean I mapped out everything; it just means I have a good starting point."

He cocks one eyebrow. "Oh, yeah? And what's that?"

"Well, first, you need to hand over whatever drugs you have left." I stick out my hand, palm up.

His eyes rake over my arm and all the way up to my face, hesitating. This wasn't how I pictured this situation unfolding. In my dream world, this strange boy would admit he has a problem and conquer his deepest, darkest fears by gladly handing over the last of his supply, thanking me in the process. Okay, it's a bit far-fetched, but it's a start, right?

"Nu-uh. No way. Not gonna happen," he responds. "You can't just take my shit."

I almost chuckle. "You're really paranoid about people confiscating your belongings, aren't you?"

Daggers virtually shoot from his eyeballs.

"Look, I don't want to touch anything that you own; I just want to help," I persist. "And the first step, I think, is wrecking your stash. Then, we'll go from there. How does that sound?"

"Horrible! You can't just take things from me and expect me to be okay with it. Because that's just it—it's *not* okay. If this is all you've thought of to help me, then don't bother. I can find help—*real* help—elsewhere." He stomps off in the direction he normally takes, one that I'm becoming quite familiar with.

"Fine," I call behind him. "Leave like you always do,

because that's really going to aid your dilemma. I'm sure it makes the pain go away, too. Maybe even acts as an emotional crutch when you need it most."

That stops him dead in his tracks. He then backs up a couple of steps and turns toward me, advancing. The look in his eyes burns with fury. *Rage.* Before I run the other way, he reaches out and seizes my slender arm. I struggle to wrench myself out of his grasp, but it's too tight.

He leans in, so close to me his breath warms my nose, and says through gritted teeth, "They provide none of the above, permanently. Temporarily, yes. It's an escape, a place I seek when my problems become too much. You have *no* idea what it's like. You live here, in your precious lake-side cottage, with the perfect family and the perfect life, while I'm struggling to live. Don't pretend you care. You don't know how."

My eyes sting with unwanted tears and it takes great effort to restrain them. This is definitely not how I dreamt this conversation. "You're wrong," I say, still attempting to worm my way out of his grip and steady my trembling voice, "on so many levels. My life is as far from perfect as it gets, and it's crumbled into nothing more than dirt." My courage falters, so I hurry to recapture it. "I have an escape, too, something that doesn't require injecting volatile substances and harming those who care for me. If I can do it, so can you."

"Oh, really? What's that, listening to music in your iPod, maybe even watching romantic comedies in the comfort of your home, cuddled up against your boyfriend?"

"No." Choosing not to inform him I haven't had a boyfriend since, oh, *never*, I reply, "I like to run."

This poor, poor boy. *What has life done to you?* Not only does he not trust me, but he's scared I'll take his belongings, and he's under the assumption my life is perfect. Maybe my family gives off that vibe, but the truth is that my parents will probably sell the summer house once they divorce. The truth is I'll probably never return to Sandy Shores due to the painful memories that occurred here. The truth is I don't know what happens next, and I'm terrified.

And damn it if I don't sniffle, totally giving away my emotions. *You betrayed me, body and mind!* He releases his hold. Still within arm's reach, he cautiously searches my face, his gaze roving all over, from eyes to nose to lips . . .

I inhale a deep breath and close my eyes. "Okay, so we don't really trust each other yet. That's fine, but how can we change?" Stealing a glance up at him, I notice his features are less severe.

"I don't know," he says finally, looking even more distraught, like it pains him to speak about this. Like he doesn't really want my help.

Wiping my eyes, I say, "Well, I think we need to figure out the basics: where you're staying, when to meet up, stuff we can mutually agree on. I don't want this to be one-sided." *Please, please, please don't back out of this.*

"I can do the basics, I guess." Surprisingly, he extends his hand and says, "Hi, I'm Logan."

A gradual smile crosses my mouth. Maybe he isn't a lost cause, after all. "Hi, Logan. I'm Chloe."

The truth is . . . I don't want to be alone anymore.

five • Chloe

"Tell me about what you were like before," I say, plucking blades of grass and tossing them at the water.

"Before?" Logan's lain back, resting on his elbows. We've been sitting for hours, waiting on the moon to rise and cast its pearlescent glow on the lake. Ripples steadily lap against the shore.

"Yeah. Like, what did you do before you . . . before you ended up like, you know . . .?"

"This?" he finishes, smoothly waving at himself.

I nod.

"I played football, mostly. Quarterback." He stares straight ahead, his face a blank canvas in which I want to paint a smile, or any emotion. "My dad always pushed me to be the best quarterback our town had seen in years. But the more pressure he and my coaches applied, the more I struggled, and the more I failed. My arm gave out mid-season—tore my rotator cuff—and I was out just like that." He snaps his fingers once for emphasis. "After I was benched, some of my fellow teammates said they had a miracle cure for the pain. They told me if I started taking morphine, I'd be back to normal in no time at all, that I'd be playing again before the season was over." He shakes his head, brusquely exhaling. "You see what good that did."

"And you blame them for getting you hooked?"

"I blame them, I blame my father, I blame my coaches—the list goes on and on."

"But not yourself?"

He snaps his head in my direction, his face warping in irritation. "Of course not. How was I supposed to know I'd become addicted to the one thing they promised would help my situation?"

I ignore his outburst, figuring he doesn't need somebody to argue with; he needs somebody who will listen. "So, tell me, is morphine what you're addicted to now?"

His body relaxes a little, as do his features. "No."

I wait and wait and wait for more information, but he doesn't deliver. God knows I don't want to get him riled up again. If there's one thing Logan needs besides rehab, it's anger management.

"I've got to head out. If your parents weren't worried about you earlier, they probably are now," he says.

"Doubt it." We spend a moment in silence. "When will I see you again?" I'm surprised at how my voice barely registers.

"I'll stop by in the next couple of days, or something." He shrugs.

Ouch. He's obviously not impressed with my rehabilitation skills.

We stand and awkwardly gaze at each other, unsure how to say goodbye.

"Until next time," I say.

"Yep. See ya."

As I watch him walk in the opposite direction, I can't help but mentally fist pump and pat myself on the back. Though it doesn't seem like I got very far, some deeper part of me shrieks, *Yes, you did!* Not only did I learn his name, but he also gave me a little glimpse of his world, why he turned out the way he is. That's something, right?

Back home, Mom's passed out on the couch and the TV screen casts eerie flashes across the walls in the living room.

"C'mon," I say, pulling the throw off her. "Let's get you tucked in."

She shakes her head, still asleep. "He has to be there. He has to." Her words trail off into nothing more than a hoarse whisper.

I frown. "Who? Dad?"

Just the mention of him brings a smile to her face, even while she's dreaming.

"Okay, Mom. He's waiting for you in bed. Let's get you upstairs." Truth is . . . it's very unlikely my father is waiting on my mom. He's probably out painting the town and won't be back until tomorrow. Nevertheless, I loop Mom's arm around my neck and pull her up. She's dead weight as I help her to the master suite, and we both stumble twice on the staircase. But once we reach her bedroom, she easily collapses on the mattress. I pull the comforter and sheet down then up, tucking her in.

And I was right—Dad's not here.

"Night, Mom. Sleep well," I whisper.

She mumbles incoherently.

Downstairs, I rummage through the refrigerator, settling on bottled water and a bag of cheese cubes. As I meander to the couch, the knob on the front door rattles. Keys jingle on the opposite side. Let's hope I don't have to help his drunken ass to bed, too—that would be the proverbial icing on top of the babysitting cake.

"Oh, uh . . . hey, pumpkin," says Dad, who doesn't look half as smashed as I thought he would.

"Late night at the office?" I finally sit down, snatching the remote from the arm of the couch, and flip through TV channels. This late, nothing's on, but it gives me something to do, as opposed to looking my dad in the eye.

"No, uh, just out with Dan. Catching up and stuff."

Jeez, can you lay off the stammering a little? It almost makes you, you know, sound like a liar.

"That's cool."

"Is your mother in bed?"

Keeping my eyes fixed on the TV screen, I reply, "Yes, Dad, your *wife* is in bed."

He's immobile on the foyer. "So, uh, I take it she's had another one of her nights?"

This time, I glare at him, hoping he'll get the message. "Of course she had one of her nights. But what do you expect when her husband does everything he can to avoid her?"

"That's not true," he says, stepping a few feet forward. "It's just . . . your mother and I . . . we're two different people now than we were twenty years ago. Things change. *People* change. That's a way of life, I guess." His fingers drag through his chestnut-colored hair. Suddenly, I'm glad I inherited my mom's blonde tresses and most of her genetics. Is that a horrible thing for me to say, because I don't want to be associated with my dad?

"Whatever happened to 'till death do us part' along with the rest of your wedding vows?" I question. "Do they mean nothing to you?"

He progressively moves to stand behind me. Leaning over the back of the couch, I now smell the stench of beer laden on his breath, floating like a thick fog between us. "We meant every word at the time. But, until you're married for a couple of decades, you have no idea what it's like."

49

I swivel on the seat cushion. "So, tell me what it's like, Dad. I'm all ears. Tell me . . . Is it absolutely horrifying, loving somebody until your bones ache, because you feel that deeply for them? Or maybe it was horrible because you two were so young when you had me and things were just never the same again." *Oh, no.* Word vomit is about to detonate in T-minus 3 . . . 2 . . . 1 . . . "Or *maybe* it's because you didn't love her enough and that's why you're having an affair!" God, I've done it now.

Dad looks like I slapped him—not once, but possibly three or four times. "How'd you . . ." he trails off. "You know, then?"

"Dad, seriously, I wasn't born yesterday, and it's not like you're double-oh-seven about it, either. The worst part? I'm positive Mom knows, too. So you're basically contributing to her drinking problem. Way to go. You deserve a freaking cookie."

"You listen to me, young lady." He growls, latching onto my arm and squeezing a bit too hard. "You don't know anything. And don't ever speak to me like that again, not under my roof!"

It's the alcohol speaking, because my dad has never grabbed me before. "Let go!" I screech, which only makes his fingers dig in harder.

"You don't disrespect me, and you don't disrespect your mother, you hear me? I'll teach you a lesson you'll never forget, so help me . . ." He tugs me over the back of the couch and drops me onto the floor with a loud *thwack*. I attempt to scurry away, like a rat looking for a hiding place, but he grabs my ankles and pulls me toward him.

Tiny pinpricks stab my eyes as tears begin to form. I'm not sure what's worse—the mental pain of my dad being so callous, or the physical pain he's causing my body. Or is it fear? Fear of the unknown.

"Get your hands off her, you son of a bitch!" Mom shouts from the top of the stairs.

Dad glances from Mom to his hands, like he's grown an extra finger on each, and then frees me from his bond. "I—I didn't mean . . . I'm sorry, Chloe," he says, shaking his head in disbelief.

Mom bounds down the stairs—a little clumsily in her condition—with a baseball bat attached to one hand and a violent look in her eyes. "You sick bastard. How dare you!"

It's then I realize how soaking wet my face is. Managing to slip out, I make it to the kitchen before I crumple into a heap on the floor. Mom and Dad's vicious screams wage back and forth across the room. I curl up into a tight ball, pulling my knees to my chin, and sob like a small child.

How *could* he? I've always read about domestic situations, but never dreamed my own father would pull a stunt like this. He was always the supportive type, the one who took my side more than Mom. But now? He's a shadow of the man I thought he was. A ghost of what he could've been. Cheating and alcohol will do that to a person, I guess.

The front door slams shut, rattling the house. Mom's at my side, soothing me, cooing in my ear, "Everything will be all right, sweetie. You and I are going to be all right."

"Will we, Mom?" I want to say, but the words suffocate in my throat, lost forever.

Her hand smoothes my hair over and over again. Eventually, she coaxes me to my bedroom, where this time, she's the one tucking *me* in.

"I'm going to make everything all right, baby. I promise." And with that, she leaves.

There's a tug in my mind, pushing a thought forward, explaining I bring nothing but bad luck, that I might be the worst person in the world. I can't help my parents. I can't help Logan. Right now, I can't even help myself. So, I cry.

And cry and cry and cry.

Six • Logan

Well, that didn't go nearly as bad as I expected. She's likeable. Cute. She does this thing with her nose where it scrunches up, and I'm convinced she doesn't even realize she's doing it. She definitely hasn't figured me out, which is a good thing—because the moment I let her in is the moment my whole charade is up. I can't let her get close; I'm practically plagued.

My plan is to let this girl have some fun this summer, since it's obvious she doesn't have any friends here. Once she returns home, I'll go back to being me, and she'll forget I ever existed. Easy enough, right?

Except, for whatever reason, I can't stop thinking about her changing me.

My mind is a traitor: *So what if she changes you? Let her.*

But that's not how it's supposed to work, I think. She has a life of her own somewhere else and can't be bothered by me. Once upon a time, she and I would've been a perfect match: cute blonde dating the all-American quarterback.

But that was before.

And, from what it sounded like, she's got enough problems on her plate without dealing with mine, too. She's not equipped to handle all the shitty baggage I carry, so there's absolutely no reason for her to get involved more than she should. Which is why I continue to revert to my original plan, the one my mind fights against.

Walking back to Bernie's, I decide to take a detour. Maybe if I stick to back roads and forgotten alleyways, Big P and his thugs won't find me. I snort. *Yeah, right.* Sometimes I wonder if those guys have a special honing device with my name on it.

I pass by the intersection I ran through earlier to escape from B and Ice. The day crowd has thinned out, and the night crowd is moving in on their territory. Loud music blares from too many speakers, pulsing tunes so hard it vibrates car frames. Girls sex up their look with heavy makeup and barely-there clothing. Guys wear sunglasses . . . at night. *Cool, bro. Really fucking badass.* I feel sorry for anyone else stuck in that mix; they don't know what they're getting themselves into. It's a maze of teenagers and college-aged kids with suped-up, low-riding vehicles their parents doled out money for because their child was too damn busy acting cool instead of getting a job.

There's a word for these kids: *wannabes*.

And if a crisis ever occurred, their parents would be the first people they call.

I shake my head, my hair swishing at eye level. Thank God my parents didn't leave a silver spoon anywhere near my mouth, because if they did, I'd be hanging out with the likes of those dudes behind me.

Crossing the parking lot behind Bernie's, I notice a guy slumped against the brick wall, facing away from me. There are only two lights in the vicinity, and neither of them is close enough to shed clarity on this homeless guy.

"Hey, man, you all right?" I ask, checking to see if he's just another drunk. Most drunks pass out, can't be awakened, and are tough to move.

And this one definitely isn't moving.

"Bro, you all right?" I ask again, moving closer. I grab his shirt sleeve and tug. His body rolls toward me enough that I see the dreads. *Oh, no.* "Jake? Can you hear me? Jake, wake up!" "Jake, Jake, JAKE," I call over and over again . . . and over and over again I don't receive a response. *He's blacked out from his run-in with Big P earlier, that's all*, I tell myself. Deep down, my stomach clenches, as if it knows this isn't normal. This isn't something that happens after you get a beat down.

I take one step to the left and a beam of light from the

parking lot illuminates Jake's face. I wish I hadn't. Jake's eyes are wide open, staring at nothing.

Blank. Void. Dead.

But his eyes aren't the worst part. The knife handle securely frozen against his stomach is, and it doesn't catch my attention as much as the piece of paper pinned underneath. *Holy shit.* Jake's abdomen was used as a bulletin board. I have to bite my tongue from screaming for help. Fresh tears nip the backs of my eyeballs, and I refuse to let them fall. He didn't deserve this.

I should be running to the police by now, running and never looking back. *Let them deal with his murder*, my conscience says. But the note is calling my name, begging me to read it. Hesitantly, I pluck the paper loose from the knife, find some light, and read.

Bring me the money, or you're next.

P

Damn, it was meant for my eyes. Why didn't he just sign it "Big P?" *Because that would make him too easy to find.* Of course he wouldn't leave a literal paper trail back to his place. So, instead, he leaves a real initial, just in case the police, or someone else, found Jake before I did.

I have absolutely no idea how I'll come up with the money I owe him. I already know what the amount is: five G's. Five fucking G's. How does a homeless guy locate that much money?

The answer is simple: he doesn't. He's offed, axed, fucked, erased—whatever one wants to call it. I need five thousand dollars, or I'll end up like Jake.

Briefly, Lucas's face flashes across my mind, and I *know* I can't die; he needs me to be his big brother. He needs me to watch out for him, to have his back, to just . . . be there. If I don't get my shit straightened out, I'll never see Lucas or my parents again. The thought sickens me. Because right now, these are the only people who matter in my life, the only people who care what happens to me. And Charlie—he cared enough to stop me the other day. Maybe that's who I should contact right now, to take care of Jake. The station is only a few blocks from here, but with Big P out and about, I don't want to be discovered.

Jake deserved so much more. He stood up for me, so it's only right that I stand up for him.

Think, Logan, think.

I crumple the note and shove it in my pocket. I'm pretty sure fucking with evidence at a crime scene is illegal in every country of the world, but I don't want the police investigation to drag out due to me. Jake needs to return home to his family, and they need to bury him. If the police see the note, Jake's body will be stuck in autopsy for days, maybe weeks, and the police may not release him until they collect all evidence. I'm doing the right thing. At least, for now. This may bite me in the ass in the future, but I can't think about that.

An anonymous call should tip the cops, which will work out

perfectly. I can be back at the cottage before they arrive. Long gone, and out of sight.

"Rest in peace, my friend," I say to Jake, and then head to the nearest payphone. The whole way I constantly glance over my shoulder, afraid of Big P showing up. Afraid he may be nearby and fuck with Jake's body before the police arrive.

There's a payphone a little past the intersection and down the street, and I don't have a view of Bernie's parking lot anymore. I dial the only three digits that can help Jake now.

"9-1-1. What's your emergency?"

"I'd like to report a murder."

Seven • Chloe

"Can you believe it?" Mom shakes her head, *tsking* the TV screen. "Sandy Shores harbors a murderer. So unexpected."

"Mom, every city harbors a murderer, even the small ones," I say, sipping the lemonade she made for me.

"But not here, Chloe, not like this. Sandy Shores is known for its low crime rate and clean town. That's why people like to vacation here; it's safe." She shakes her head again and returns to the kitchen. "Do you want another after that?" Mom asks, nodding toward my cup.

"Oh, no. I'm fine, thanks."

She returns to the living room with her coffee mug in hand

and sits down on the opposite end of the couch from me. Since Dad's outburst last night, she's refrained from wine or anti-depressants; instead, catering to my every need. It's almost smothering. I know she means well—she's just worried about me—but really, I'm okay. Yes, it was freaky and scary and I hope I never have to deal with my dad again, but I'll pull through. It could've been *a lot* worse, but the point is, it wasn't.

"I want you to stay inside until they find this killer," says Mom.

Uhhh . . . no can do. "I can't even go to the lake, which is, like, five feet from our house?"

"It's much more than five feet, Chloe. And no, I'm forbidding you to go anywhere until they have this lunatic in custody."

I discharge a frustrated sigh. "You can't keep me on lockdown. That's not fair."

"It's not fair that somebody lost their life last night, either."

Gahhh. She always does that—makes me think on a deeper level than what I'm used to. Makes me feel sorry for the person I'm supposed to feel sorry for, and myself, for misplacing my caring heart every once in a while.

Then a thought strikes me: what if that homeless guy was Logan? What if he's zipped up in a body bag at the morgue? What if I'm sitting here, sipping my freshly-prepared lemonade while he sleeps forever?

"Did they, uh, did they say who died?" I ask.

"They haven't released his name yet." She glances at me, sees the color leave my face, I'm sure. "Why? What's wrong?"

"I need some fresh air," I reply.

"Oh, no you don't. Crack your window if you need it that badly."

"Fine," I say. "I'll crack a window." Doesn't she know I can easily slide down the lattice by our back porch if I wanted out?

All craziness aside, that dead boy might be Logan. I mean, what if he ran into the wrong crowd last night after he saw me and they did this to him? My stomach rolls over. This is not good. I can't leave the house, I can't go searching for him, and I don't know what the name of the dead guy is.

Worst. Summer. Ever.

I open the window wide enough to stick my head out. I can't breathe anymore, it seems like. Sandwiched between parents who hate each other and the fact that Logan might be dead, my throat feels like it is closing. Like, it physically wants to suffocate itself. How does that work?

I glimpse at the lake. Bright reflections of the sun glisten on the water, tourists steadily float downstream in fishing boats, and our neighbors two doors down eat breakfast at a small table on the lake's edge. It's way too early for me to be up during summer vacation, but this hasn't exactly been a normal trip.

"Hey, Rapunzel, let down your hair," the all-too-familiar voice calls from below. I just glare at him, at *Logan*. "Okay, fine," he says. "I'll come up."

I'm too stunned to say anything. He's alive? He's . . . alive. *He's here, climbing up the lattice like he's Prince Charming, rescuing a damsel in distress.* Am I a damsel in distress? It's quite possible these days since my stress level is way out there. He throws his backpack on the patio's miniature roof as he finishes the climb to me. I step back to let him in.

Slightly out of breath, he says, "What? You're not happy to see me?" He grins, but that fades when he sees my face. "What's wrong?"

"It wasn't you," I say, and then slam into him, full force. This might be totally inappropriate, but who cares? I'm just happy he's here.

His arms falter before finally circling around my waist, his chin resting atop my head. "No," he says, "it wasn't me. But I knew the guy."

I pull back to look up at him. "I'm sorry to hear that. Were you close?"

He shrugs. "You could say that."

Rushing over to my bedroom door, I lock it. There's a sudden thrill coursing through my body, reminding me this is completely outlawed. If my mom catches Logan up here, he'll be dead.

"Hey, keep quiet," I say as Logan collapses onto my bed. "If my mom hears any added noise up here, she'll be suspicious."

Logan wiggles his fingers in the air and says, "Ooooh. I'm so scared."

Hands on hips, I retort, "What's with you this morning?"

"What do you mean?" he asks, resting on his elbows.

"You're too . . . happy." I frown; that doesn't seem right. He just lost his friend in a murder and he's up early *and* he climbed up to my window to see me. This guy has yet to be glad to see me. Even during our brief meetings he finds ways to avoid looking at me, or he cuts the meeting short. I narrow my eyes. "What's *really* with you? I mean, did you shoot up, or whatever it's called, this morning?"

He pushes off his elbows and sits at the edge of my bed. "You think I can't just be happy for once?"

"No, I'm not say—"

"That because I'm a depressed, homeless, drug-addicted guy, there's no possible way for me to ever have feelings again? That I'm forever stuck in this shitty limbo of needles, permanent roaming, and scavenging for food? Is that what you think?"

I shake my head and hiss, "Keep it down."

He bolts off my bed and crosses the room. I let out a tiny squeal as he pushes me against the wall and covers my mouth with his hand. "Quiet," he whispers, pressing his body against mine. There's nothing separating the two of us but clothes, and I feel the heat radiating from his skin. "I have news for you, Chloe: I won't always be a horrible guy. One day I'll go back to being me, but until then, I am stuck in my own personal purgatory, tortured by demons you can't imagine."

He removes his hand, our lips only inches apart. I refrain

from closing the distance between us, knowing it's wrong; I set out to assist the guy, not torture him even more.

"I'll help you, but you have to trust me," I tell him, my chest rising and falling with irregular breaths. "I can't do this if you aren't on board one hundred percent, got it?"

He nods.

"First things first, take a shower," I say, pushing him off me and wrinkling my nose for an added effect. He blushes a little. "Oh, don't be embarrassed. I'm not judging you; I know you can't help it. Now, go." I hold out my arm, pointing toward the bathroom. "When you're finished, I'll wash your clothes."

"You don't have to do this, you know," he says.

"We have an agreement, don't we? I'm not going to let you just . . . rot."

His eyebrows tighten together. "So, now I'm rotting?"

"Worse," I say. "You smell like dry dirt and B.O." I emphasize this with a *yuck*. "And yes, you might be rotting on the inside. There's no telling what drugs have done to you."

"Fine," he says. "Have it your way." Without breaking eye contact, he strips off his shirt.

And his jeans.

And—*gasp!*—his boxers.

Oh, holy mother. I can't close my mouth, or avert my eyes. *Pull yourself together, Chloe!*

"Like what you see?" asks Logan, with a big, cheesy grin on his face.

"Just . . . shoo!" I turn my head away and wave toward the bathroom.

Logan laughs, deep and throaty. "You don't want to join me?"

Don't tempt me, son of Aphrodite! "Um, no." I clear my throat. "Maybe some other time."

"I'll hold you to that," he says.

I jerk my head around to face him, eyes wide. "I-I didn't mean—"

"Oh, you said it," he adds promptly. "You said it, and there's no Get-Out-of-Jail-Free card lying around, so guess what that means?"

I try swallowing the knot in my throat.

"It means your naked ass will be mine. Soon." He still has that cheap smile plastered to his face as he closes the bathroom door behind him.

Eight • Logan

What am I doing? I mean, really. I need to grab a hold of my balls and act like a fucking man, not spend my time dicking around with Chloe. She'll be gone within a couple of months, and if I don't clean up before then, well, I'm shit out of luck. No returning home and patching things up with the fam. No playing football with Lucas on the front lawn. This is my *life* we're attempting to transform. I need to stop jacking off and focus on what's important.

But Chloe is too damn intoxicating. Yeah, I guess that's the right word. Her hair smells like a cool ocean breeze and is as bright as the sun, and her curvy lips are just *begging* me to kiss them. That or it's my fucked-up mind playing tricks on me. I could've opened her mouth with mine, let my tongue discover hers. She thought about it, too. I saw the way she watched my lips hovering three inches away; she *wanted* me to kiss her.

And I'm a fucking idiot because I didn't. Instead, I had to conduct a striptease in the middle of her room and ask if she liked the view, or some shit. *Why'd you do that, Logan? Why, why, why?* asks one-half of my brain. The other half is saying, *You want her as much as she wants you. Don't stop.*

No. This ends here, in her bathroom. Odd place, I know, but if I don't stop myself now, I'm not entirely sure what will become of us later. And I don't want to ruin her friendship, especially when she's trying to help me get my old life back.

"Hey, Logan?"

I freeze. Her voice is barely audible over the running water. "Yeah?"

"I brought you a couple of towels. I'll just set them over here."

I have no idea where "here" is, but that's nice of her. "Okay, thanks."

She closes the door, and I can breathe again. Funny how five minutes ago I didn't care about showing my junk, but now I feel awkward in a shower. Probably has something to do with the fact that I've talked myself out of her pants. For now, at least.

I finish showering and dry off, wrapping a towel around my waist, and open the bathroom door, releasing the humid air. I hand Chloe my clothes, which she mixes in with her own dirty laundry so her mom won't notice.

"What about your other clothes?" she asks, nodding toward my backpack.

I shrug. "Don't worry about them."

"Okay. I'll be back," she says. She snatches a towel out of her closet and wraps it around her head. "Can't exactly walk downstairs with dry hair; that'd be tough to explain."

After she disappears, I check out her room. The walls change colors between blue and purple, and the shift between the two fades like sidewalk chalk during a rainstorm. It's a strange paint job, to say the least. She also has purple shelves attached to each wall; some hold books, some hold local souvenirs, some hold picture frames filled with memories. Those are what I scan through, seeing what her past holds. What I find saddens me, because the girl in these photographs is not the Chloe I know; the girl from the past is the real deal, smiling and laughing, and Chloe's just a shadow. The girl from the past seems happy and vivacious, and the present-day Chloe is held back by fear and unhappiness, and maybe even desperation. Chloe's reaching for something, but she doesn't know what it is just yet.

Maybe it's me. Maybe that's why she wanted to help—I'm what she's been searching for all along. The thought stops my heart for a mere second. If that's true, if fate is so fucked up as to bring us together under horrible circumstances, then she and I won't have much time together. She'll be gone in less than two months, and I'll be Godknowswhere.

"I'm back," she says, startling me. "Remind me to check on the clothes in twenty minutes or so. I don't want my mom to accidentally pick up yours and interrogate me." She rolls her eyes and unwraps the towel around her head.

I just stare at her. *Who are you?* I want to ask. *Who are you and what have you done with the real Chloe? I want to meet her, the real you.*

Instead, like the pussy that I am, I say, "Okay," and leave it at that.

"So, while you were in the shower, I came up with a few ideas," she goes on, picking up a piece of paper and sitting on the edge of her bed. "And since you won't hand over your stash, we're going to have to come up with a new plan of action."

"Oh, yeah? Like what?"

"Like, sports or outdoor activities, something that will keep your mind focused on anything but drugs." There she goes again with that nose scrunching. "You don't look so thrilled."

"Um, sure. Sports. Yeah. Totally stoked."

Shaking her head, she says, "At some point you do realize you'll have to discard whatever needles and/or paraphernalia you have on you, right? This process isn't going to work unless you go all the way."

"We'll deal with that later," I say, gritting my teeth. I don't want to think about what withdrawal will be like, for both our sakes. Right now I need to focus on how I'll be coping when the withdrawal hits me, which won't be pretty.

"All right. So," she begins, glancing over her little to-do list, "what do you think about this weekend? For starting this routine, I mean." She glances up at me, big blue eyes under thick eyelashes.

"Tomorrow," I respond. "There's no sense in waiting. I need to get in shape, and we probably won't have much time, anyway."

Puzzled, her brows crush together. "Why won't we have time?"

Go for the kill, heartbreaker. Do what you do best. "Because you'll leave in a couple of months, go back to wherever it is you came from, and we won't ever see each other again. So, that's that. The sooner we can get this over with, the sooner I can return home and we can 'part ways,'" I say, adding air quotes around the last bit.

Her head jerks back slightly, but she's quick to cover up her offended expression with a more neutral one. "All right." She even fakes a smile.

I nod.

"Um," she says, breaking our stare by glancing at her notepaper, "tomorrow it is, then. Bright and early, we'll go running. How does that sound?"

"Good."

"I'm just going to . . ." She points toward her bedroom door and smiles, partially.

"Yeah, sure, go ahead."

The door closes behind her and I want to beat the shit out of myself. How am I not going to fall for this girl over the next two months? She cute, sexy, and smart—and she has no idea she's any of these things. I bet a guy's never told her, either. Has she even been kissed? What if I'm her first?

Lose the idea, Logan. It can't happen.

But it *can* happen, and that's what I'm afraid of. I'm afraid that, for once in my life, I'll accomplish something great, I won't be a failure, and, as it always happens, that something will be ripped from my arms—and my heart, if we get that far. Because if there's one thing I've learned from our short meetings together, it's that my heart is definitely in trouble.

Chloe returns with two sandwiches and two bottles of water.

"I was trying to hurry," she murmurs. "I didn't want Mom asking why I had two of each. Fortunately, she didn't even look up from the TV."

"Well, that's good."

"Yeah, so . . . I was thinking . . ."

We sit down on her bed, and I rearrange my towel so I won't flash her like earlier, even if that was intentional. She and I need to be able to hold a serious conversation without my junk interfering as a sideshow.

"About what?"

"About your sleeping situation," she says slowly. "You don't plan on staying in the old cottage, do you?"

I lift my shoulders for a couple of seconds, and then let them fall. "I guess. I mean, I don't have anywhere else to sleep."

"That's what I thought you'd say," she says, in between bites of her sandwich. Her eyes dance, like she's up to no good. "What if I asked you to stay here and sleep in my closet? There's plenty of room."

I don't know what worries me more: the fact that I'm concerned, at first, about how much closet space she has, or the fact that I don't question staying here before I question the closet space. And if these two thoughts aren't dire enough, I actually glance toward her closet to assess the amount of room available.

She follows my line of sight and stands up. "Want me to open it?"

"Nah, that's okay." *Stay away from her, man. You guys* cannot *sleep under the same roof.*

"You sure? It'll be a lot comfier than sleeping on those wooden boards." She transfers weight from one foot to the other and clasps her hands in front. "I'm serious, Logan. Think about this. You'll have food and water and shelter, which is better than what you've had for the past . . . however long you've been living like this."

I nod. "I'll think about it, but no guarantees and no promises, got it?"

She purses her lips and nods in return. "Got it."

The next thirty minutes are spent talking about our lives, how we ended up here, where we want to go. Chloe opens up regarding her past, and I tell her little regarding mine. I know it's selfish, but I don't want her becoming attached and then toss me aside when she finds a new toy. My mind tells me Chloe's different; she won't do that. The other half of me is arguing that it doesn't matter. Once she's gone for the summer, with the way her living situation is, she'll be gone forever.

She runs downstairs to get our clothes and returns with a ball of mismatched items. Separating my clothes from hers, I actually hold mine up and sniff the fresh scent; it reminds me of home. My mom always washed laundry on weekends and, after they finished drying, she'd lay them on my bed. I've never forgotten their aroma—warm and clean, inviting me to put them on and never take them off.

It's the same way now.

Dressing in my T-shirt, boxers, and jeans, I then throw the used towel in Chloe's laundry hamper. "Well," I say, "I guess I'll see you tomorrow?"

"If that's what you want."

"It is." *For now, but you'll be thinking otherwise when you don't have any H left in your system,* my mind adds.

Climbing out the way I came in, I reach ground level and glance back up at Chloe. She smiles and waves. Not the same smile I want to see on her face, but it's a smile. Walking back to the cottage, past the overgrown brush and underneath the sun's heated gaze, I secretly wish I agreed to sleep in her closet.

Nine • Chloe

On my jog over to the cottage, the sun already blazes on my face and arms, and the tourists and locals are taking advantage of this fact by hanging out on the river. Two people zip across the water on jet skis, spraying anyone within range. A third person on a jet ski has an inner tube attached, with a girl lounging in it.

"Ready?" I hear the man call to the girl in the oversized, black donut.

"Ready!" she replies, followed by a screech of anticipation.

The man takes off slowly, but eventually increases his speed, and the girl in the inner tube screams as they whiz down the lake. I grin and shake my head. Must be nice, having the luxury of spending all day on the water. I had hoped my parents would take our boat out one last time, but that's obviously not going to happen. I'm sure Dad will sell it once their divorce is finalized.

As I enter the cottage, I notice Logan is curled up in his usual corner, sweating profusely, hugging his knees to his chest.

"Oh, my God. Logan? Logan!" His eyes stare past me, to nothing. Racing to him, and careful to avoid any holes in the floor, I shove him a little, just to see if he responds. As if he's caught in slow motion, he lifts one fist, turns it palm up, and unwraps his clenched fingers.

"Take it," he says in a gust. "Take it and bury it somewhere so I'll never find it."

I glance at the objects: two needles, a bag of I-don't-want-to-know-what's-in-there, a spoon, and a pipe. All items are protected with balled-up newspaper scraps, like a cushion, and placed in a plastic sandwich bag.

He's handing over his stash! Step one is complete. I snatch the bag from him and take off toward the woods by the cottage. Without tools to dig a hole, I'll have to use my fingers. It'll be worth it, though, especially if this means Logan is forever freed from his drug addiction.

I run and run and run until I'm completely out of breath. Just in case he changes his mind and decides to follow me, I need to hurry. There are so many trees that I don't know if I'll ever find my way back; they all look the same. I pick one, squatting down at its base and raking the soil with my fingertips. The further I tunnel into the ground, the harder and more compact the dirt becomes, which slows me down. I need Logan's stuff to be buried forever, not someplace where hikers or a passerby will stumble across it.

Finishing up, I pack the dirt, throw a few twigs and leaves on top, and begin walking back to the cottage. I'm worried about Logan. I've never seen him look like that; it must be a side effect, or he's beginning withdrawal.

He's crying when I return. So much so, his cheeks are shiny from the amount of tears staining them.

"Oh, sweetie." I sit down, pressing my hand to his forehead. He's burning up with a fever.

"Why'd you take it, Chloe? Why?" he begs and scorns simultaneously. "You shouldn't have taken it; you should've left it alone."

"What good would that have done?"

"I want it baaaaaack!" he screams. Violently, he shakes his head, his shaggy hair slinging back and forth. "Back, back, back," he repeats over and over again.

Reality check, Chloe. This is the real deal. "You're not getting it back, and I'm not telling you where it is. And if you continue to act this way, I'm leaving." I stand up, but he grabs my arm, his fingernails digging into my skin. I try to yank out of his grasp, but he squeezes tighter.

"Take me to it," he says, his eyes filling with more tears, pooling against angry, red rims. "I made a mistake. Can I *please* have it back?"

"No," I state with finality, then wrench my arm free of him. I take off running out of the cottage, headed for my house. I don't know why I run, other than the fact that he's completely off his rocker right now and I'm uncertain what he's capable of.

He catches up, though, snatching me around my waist and pulling me to the ground. When he flips me over on my back, I flail and kick, trying to push him off. We wrestle for a matter of minutes, neither one of us truly gaining control over the other, until my limbs become weak and strained. I slap him once across the face and he growls in response, clasping my wrists and pinning them above my head as he looms over me. This brings back sore memories of my dad, which are all too recent. Of course, the experience with my dad never went far, thanks to Mom, but this is still pretty damn close.

"Get off!" I scream.

"Tell. Me. Where. You. Hid. It," he articulates through gritted teeth.

I turn my head away and, pressing my eyes shut, hold on to a tiny shard of hope that Logan will return to his former self. "Please stop," I whisper. "Don't do this."

Logan doesn't move, doesn't say anything; he freezes.

I roll my head so I look up at him once more. His eyes fume, like all the anger of the world is seething behind them, unrestrained.

"Please, *please*," I plea. "I'm doing this for your own good,

Logan. You have to trust me."

Something in him shifts, like he's finally aware of his surroundings, aware of me. The fury and wrath I witnessed just a moment ago is now gone, and is replaced by fright. "Jesus, Chloe. I'm sorry." Freeing my wrists, he tugs me into his arms, onto his lap. I rest my head on his shoulder, and he rubs my back. "I'm so sorry. I-I didn't . . . I wasn't thinking. I'm not *me*."

"I know," I choke out, letting a tear descend. For the first time since the incident with my dad, I want to talk to somebody about how it made me feel, about how it made me irate. "My dad attacked me the other night, so I sort of . . . froze up. I thought you might do the same."

Logan pushes me backward so he can look at me. "He fucking attacked you? How?"

Shaking my head, I glance away. "He was drunk. I pissed him off. Luckily, my mom was there to stop him." I shrug. "And that's that."

"Hell no it's not. Is that how you got the bruises on your knees?" His hands immediately slide to the bend in my legs, lightly brushing his fingertips across my skin, searing my flesh with his touch. I shiver and close my eyes, savoring the sensation. "Tell me, damn it!" He literally shakes me out of my musing.

Hoarsely, I respond, "Yes."

Pressing his lips to my forehead, he makes a gruff, throaty sound. "I'm sorry that happened to you. If I could find a way to fix it, if I could knock some sense into him, I'd do it."

I swallow back the burning lump in my throat. "I'll be fine. It was just . . . unexpected. He's never done something like that before."

"Well, he should've never crossed the line, no matter how much he'd been drinking."

"If my mom hadn't been there, I don't know what would've happened."

He pulls me to his chest. "I'm glad she was." Wrapping one arm around my waist, he resumes languorous loops across my back with his fingers. "Do you know what you do to me?" he whispers against my ear, catching me by surprise.

My heart speeds up, and my mind isn't within reason. So, I shake my head.

"I can't stop thinking about you," he goes on, "but I know if I become attached, you'll be taken from me. Like, this is too good to be true." He takes a few ragged breaths, and then presses his brow to mine. "Everything I've ever cared about has disappeared from my life. I don't want the same to happen with you."

"It won't," I say, but I can't make promises. Truth: he's right. In a couple of months, I'll be leaving, heading back home, and I'm not sure what will happen to Logan, or *us*.

He groans. "Don't fucking lie to me, Chloe. I'm serious. I don't want to lose you. You're the first good thing to happen to me in a long, long time."

"I wouldn't lie to you, Logan," I say. "Not about something

like this."

A gleam sparks in his eyes at my response. He murmurs, "What do we do now? Where do we go from here?"

"Well, first, we can go back to my place, where you'll be staying until we can figure something out. Your friend's murderer is still out there, somewhere, and I don't want you all alone."

His thumb grazes my cheek. "I'm capable of defending myself."

"I didn't say you weren't," I reply, "but I worry when you're out here. You need food and a roof over your head and . . . me." I blatantly grin.

"You, huh?"

"Yes, me."

"Yes, you," he agrees.

"So it's settled, then?" I raise my eyebrows and cross my arms, challenging him to say he can't stay at my house.

He takes the bait. "All right. I'll sleep in your closet."

After Logan gathers his backpack, we amble to the lake house. I enter through the sliding glass doors at the rear, and Logan climbs up to the second floor, to my bedroom window.

"I'm going to run to the grocery store tomorrow. Is there anything you want?" Mom asks as I pass by the living room on my way upstairs.

"Uhhh," I stammer, stepping back one stair, "nothing I can think of right now. I'll let you know?"

She nods. "Oh, and Chloe," she says, stopping me again. "I've thought about it, and if you want to go to the police station and file a restraining order, let me know."

"Restraining order? For what?"

"For your father, of course." She narrows her eyes. "Why else?"

I let my shoulders fall. "Mom, I understand you're looking out for me, but Dad was drunk. It was a one-time thing in the eighteen years I've been alive, and I just don't see him as a threat."

She purses her lips. "Fine. But if you change your mind . . ."

"I know."

She returns to the TV, and I return to my room, which I haven't been more excited to see than now. If the butterflies in my stomach are any indication, then Logan is the only positive thing to come out of this summer. He may also be the most destructive.

I close the bedroom door behind me, sprinting across my room to flip the latch and open my window. "Sorry, got sidetracked by my mom."

"No worries," he says, sliding one leg, then another, through the opening.

"I'm going to grab some extra sheets and pillows so you can fix your bed." I add, "I wish we had an air mattress."

"That's okay," says Logan. "This is better than rotted wooden boards, bugs crawling across my body, and mustiness."

He smiles genuinely.

Searching our linen closet in the hallway upstairs, I find a couple of extra sets of sheets, as well as one extra pillow—not two like I had hoped for, but it's better than nothing. Logan creates his spare bed, while I manage to sneak more food from the kitchen.

"I hope you don't mind," he says when I return. He sits on the edge of my bed, flipping through channels on my television. "It's just . . . I don't remember the last time I watched TV."

"Of course I don't mind. Watch whatever you want to."

He settles down, with his back against the wall, selecting an action flick. I double check that my bedroom door is locked, and then curl up next to him, smelling a mixture of both mold and laundry detergent on his clothes.

"I like this," Logan says, rubbing his hand up and down my arm. His touch spreads tingling warmth under my skin and into my abdomen. "It reminds me of home."

"Why?"

"Because it's clean and safe."

Okay, there's really nothing to say to that. He's been bouncing from abandoned houses to empty alleyways for months now and this is bringing back memories. Good memories. Maybe I underestimated myself when I took him on as a project. I mean, if I'm being honest, the guy isn't some drone from an alien planet; he's a human being, with feelings. So all of this homeliness may be exactly what he needs for his rehabilitation

82

process.

Crossing my fingers.

~~~

"Don't touch her!"

The words pull me out of my sleep. My first thought: *Oh, God, my dad's back.* I jump out of bed and turn on my light. Glancing around my room, I don't see anything. Logan repeats himself, and that's when I realize he's having a nightmare.

"Don't touch her! Don't fucking touch her, I said!"

"Logan, sweetie," I murmur, gently tugging on his upper arm. "Logan, it's me . . . Chloe. You're dreaming."

He breathes rapidly in and out of his nose, like he's hyperventilating, and he's not waking up. If my mom hears him, she won't hesitate to throw him out, and then we'll be back at square one. So, I do the only thing that pops into my mind: I kiss him.

He struggles at first, but then his body relaxes. I pull back when his eyelids open.

"Chloe," he whispers.

"You were having a nightmare."

He wraps one arm around my waist and drags me on top of him. I bury my face in his neck, sighing contentedly. Slowly, he runs his hands underneath my shirt, across my ribs, and back down. A moderate fire swells where his fingers stroke; it filters deep into my stomach, settling at the bottom.

"I'm sorry I woke you up," he says.

"What were you dreaming about?"

His Adam's apple bobs as he swallows hard. "You."

Ten • Chloe

I can't believe we slept together last night. Okay, not *slept together*, slept together. We kept it clean. The fact that my mom didn't check on me was a relief, too. When we woke this morning, Mom was nowhere to be found. I washed the rest of Logan's clothes, and then we ate breakfast, deciding we'll take a jog, maybe do a little swimming. Later, we'll come back here, shower, and crash.

"Can I be honest with you?" Logan asks between breaths. We've been jogging next to the lake for the past ten minutes.

"I would hope so," I respond, squinting at the early-morning sun intensifying on the horizon.

"Okay," he begins, taking a deep breath. "I don't know if this is going to work."

I stop running. "Don't tell me you're backing out, especially after your episode yesterday. Logan, you know what drugs have done to you. You've lost your family, friends, potential football career . . . the list goes on and on. Yet you still want *more*, as if you haven't hurt yourself and those you love enough already."

He glances away, resting his hands atop his head, jaw flexing and relaxing. "Have you ever wanted something so badly, but you just *know* it's not good for you?"

"Yes," I mumble, thinking about how many boys I've had crushes on, only to have them break my heart by rejection. In the end, something inside told me they weren't the person I thought they were.

"Well, that's how I feel about heroin." *So that's his drug of choice.* Until now, he had only mentioned an addiction to morphine, but I remember hearing that heroin is derived from morphine. Makes sense, because of his football injuries. "And I know this is probably over your head," he continues, "but this is what matters to me, because for over six months now, I haven't known anything else."

"I'm listening," I say, urging him to get this off his chest, especially if this means he'll come to terms with the fact that he has a serious problem. Because, right now, it sounds like he's trying to back out of this treatment plan. And if that's the case, I don't think I'll stick around for him much longer. This can't be a toss-up; I can't go back and forth. He either wants my help or he doesn't. It's as simple as that.

His hands fall beside him, and he can't stand still, pacing in circles, hands shifting from his hips to his sides again and again. "Okay, this may sound cheesy, but it's the only way I can tell you so that it makes sense."

He waits for my . . . approval, I guess? I nod.

"Heroin is like my girl. She can be a complete bitch, but when we're good, we're really fucking good. Unnaturally, of course. I'm completely attached to her, and she's my obsession." He glances my way. "Does this make any sense?"

"Yeah, keep going."

"So, when she was taken from me—"

I hold up one finger. "Um, correction: she wasn't *taken* from you. You freely gave her away. I'm not into thievery, just so we're clear."

"Okay, fine. I gave her up. But the point is she left. She's gone, and I can't do anything about it. I almost feel like my insides are crumbling into tiny pieces, like aged buildings before they finally collapse. My heart feels like it's been ripped from my chest, only to be replaced again every time I look at you." That really gets my attention. I jerk my head toward him, but he's oblivious to what he just said, I think. "And now that she's gone forever, I miss her. I don't know if I made the right choice. So, naturally, I'm torn."

"You *know* you did the right thing, but you also have the itch to use again. I get it."

He bares his teeth. "And damn it, I feel like I want to murder somebody right now, maybe even take a few hostages. I feel like crying and screaming at the same time. I'm so conflicted. My brain is in chaos."

I close the distance between us and wrap my arms around his waist, laying my cheek against his chest. "You're going to be all right," I say. "I promise I'll help you get through your wild emotions."

He sighs and encircles me with his arms. "Seriously, if you hadn't come along when you did, I might be dead right now." Then, faintly, he adds, "I might be in Jake's place."

"Let's not think about that, all right?" I mumble against his shirt. "Let's think happy thoughts, like gradually getting you involved with your family again. That's my next plan of action."

He chuckles, and the sound rumbles against my ear. "So that's next on the to-do list?"

"Mmm-hmm."

"And after that?"

Peering up at him, I answer, "Haven't gotten that far yet, but I'm working on it."

Logan gets this roguish look on his face as he gazes out at the lake. "I know what we can do next," he says.

Before I can ask what he's talking about, he picks me up and slings me over his shoulder. I squeal and yell, "Put me down!" even though I know it's useless. He wades through the shallow part of the lake's edge, and then, when the water level is up to his waist, he tosses me like a ping-pong ball in a beer pong match, easily and effectively, liquid splashing all around me as I hit the surface.

"Logan!" I screech as I come up for air. "How could you?"

"What?" He shrugs. "It's already hot out. That shit back there was getting too intense, so I decided to cool us down." His grin is so wide, his cheeks probably hurt.

"Oh, that's it," I say, splashing my way over to him and dunking his head.

We play fight, dipping each other, lurking underwater so the other doesn't know where we'll pop up next. Pretending we're Olympic swimmers, we practice our backstrokes, and then float atop the water, allowing the lake to carry us where it sees fit.

Logan and I swim until our muscles ache and our stomachs grumble from lack of food. Drenched, we walk back to the lake house, where I'm sure my mom has returned from wherever she decided to go earlier. I take one glance at Logan and realize his face is pale—not what it should be after being in the sun all morning.

"Are you okay?" I ask.

He lifts his eyes. "I don't know. I don't feel well."

"It looks like the blood has drained from your face." I circle his waist with my arm. He leans on me a little, but not so I'm supporting his full weight. "You're probably exhausted. I mean, we didn't sleep at all last night, and we've been swimming. Your body's not used to it."

"Probably," he says.

I release him when we reach the house so he can climb up to my window. Mom's eating a sandwich and chips in the living room, while flipping through channels.

"Hey, baby," she says. "I got groceries this morning, so we have plenty of snacks."

"Cool." I dart past her and up the stairs.

"Chloe," she presses, "why are you soaking wet?"

Think, Mom. Why else? "I went swimming."

She pauses. "Are you okay, honey? I'm really worried about you."

I lean against the banister and sigh. "I'm fine. Why?"

"You spend all your time locked up in your room. It doesn't seem normal. You weren't that way before you father . . ." she trails off.

"Mom! I'm fine, okay? This has nothing to do with Dad. I'm just bored out of my mind and don't want to deal with either of you until the divorce is finalized."

She stops chewing, holding a chip in mid-air. "Your father and I won't start the paperwork until we return home. As far as I know, he's gone back, so it's just us. I thought we might enjoy the lake house one last time."

I clear my throat. "Yeah, um, sorry. I didn't mean—"

She waves me off. "You didn't mean anything by it, I know. Now, go on and do whatever it is you're doing in your room. I still don't know if I should be worried or not."

"Definitely *not*," I say, but the truth is she'll freak if she finds Logan in my room, or hanging out at my window. In their minds, my parents have kept this clean persona of me, as I'm sure most parents do until their children reach a certain age, but that doesn't mean I'm Ms. Goodie Two Shoes. And if she knew what I've *really* been doing, well, I may never see the light of day again.

"I'm still holding you to that rain check for a movie," she calls behind me as I walk down the hallway toward my bedroom. I don't respond.

After I open the window for Logan, I grab a couple of towels so we can dry off.

"Do you want to take a shower first?" I ask, motioning with my head toward the bathroom.

"Nah. You can go."

"You sure? You still look pretty pale."

He shakes his head.

"All right," I say awkwardly, although, to be honest, I have no idea why this moment is uncomfortable. Maybe because we're discussing a shower? Maybe because I have to dig through my bra and underwear drawer in front of him? All I know is I've never done this with any boy before. Then again, Logan isn't just any boy.

As I lay my clothes out on the closed toilet lid, Logan says, "Door stays open."

I twist my head to glare at him. "What? Why?"

"You've seen me naked. Now, it's my turn to see you."

My jaw drops. "That's not fair. I didn't ask to see you naked."

Amused, he crosses his arms as he leans against the wall. "You told me to strip off my dirty clothes so you could wash them. I'm pretty sure that counts."

Rolling my eyes, I reply, "I didn't mean it like *that*; I only meant for you to get them off of you so I could be nice and help you out, like a Good Samaritan."

He tries not to smile. "Same thing."

Abruptly, Logan's face pales out. He cups his hand over his mouth and makes a mad dash to the bathroom, throwing my clothes off the toilet lid and propping it open. He vomits until I doubt he has anything left in his system and all that's coming up is stomach acid. I rush downstairs and grab a soda and crackers, hurriedly bringing it back and setting it on the bathroom countertop.

"Okay, showers can wait," I say.

"I'm fine," he says, his voice echoing in the toilet bowl.

"No, you're not. This must be some side effect of the drugs, or you've started the withdrawal process."

"I said I'm fine!"

It's pointless to argue with him when he's like this. I know it's not really him *per se*, but the other side of Logan. The mean side. The side that hates the world for the way he's been treated.

All I can do is be there for him, let him know he's not alone.

"I brought you some crackers and a drink," I tell him. "They should help your stomach feel a little better."

He waves me off. "I don't need them."

God, his mood swings are worse than a girl who's PMSing. *Be easy on him, Chloe. He doesn't realize what he's saying.* If only that were true. I'm ninety-nine percent certain that Logan is fully aware of the words coming out of his mouth. I'd hate to have to punch him again.

"Well, if you change your mind . . ." I leave him with that as I settle on my bed and turn on the TV.

He pukes a few more times, but nothing comes up; he's basically dry heaving at this point. Logan finally stands and turns on the faucet, utilizing the cold water to splash his flushed face. Using a hand towel to wipe off the excess water, he takes a moment to stare at himself in the mirror. I hate watching him. I hate feeling like I'm borderline creeper. There's just something that's fascinating about a person who looks at their reflection. What are they contemplating? Is he reminiscing about how he got to this point, about everything that's led him to the right here, right now?

Part of me thinks, *I'll never know.* The other part of me thinks, *He'll tell you, eventually. Give it time.* Except, time is what we don't have at the moment; we're stuck in an hourglass, and the sand is vanishing bit by bit.

Eleven • Logan

My eyeballs feel like they're about to pop out of my head. I've thrown up before, but this is totally different. This feels like my guts are going to slide out of my throat and into the toilet. And, of all things, I had to puke in front of Chloe. I had to wreck the flirting and teasing and what was turning into one of the best days I've had in a really, really long time. I ruined it. All of it. I'm so fucking disgusted with myself, I might puke again.

Chloe's been so nice about it, too, which makes me feel like shit. Not physically, but emotionally. The withdrawal from H has done its number on me; I can't handle anything else past this point. Right now, I want to beat the shit out of something. Maybe my fist meeting a brick wall will help. Who knows? I also have the urge to just fucking cry about everything. *Everything.* I continue to daydream about Lucas, about me being there for him when he needs me. About him trying to act cool and impress his big bro. But I'm not there; I'm here. And now I'm going through withdrawal because I was addicted to heroin. This is me. Logan Andrews. Resident low-life druggie, who can't get his shit straight.

"I can't be here," I say, nearly strangling on the words.

Chloe sits up. "What do you mean?"

"Just what I said. I. Can't. Be. Here. I need to go." Although, where and why I'm going, I'm unsure, but I have an idea, and it's not a good one. As a matter of fact, it's a piss-poor excuse of an idea. Something so far-fetched, I can't even believe I'm about to do it. But my body is caving in on itself, and I can't control these feelings any longer. The needs of my body outweigh the needs of my mind.

Chloe stands. "Logan, don't do this. I know what you're about to do. Just . . . don't."

I can't even look her in the eye. God, I'm such a horrible excuse for a human being. "Not now. I don't need your shit right now. What I need—" I stop myself. She knows. I know. There's no point in trying to explain myself.

Her bottom lip quivers, and I resist every urge to kiss it again, make it all better.

"Please," she begs.

One simple word has a dramatic effect on my heart and soul, but it's not enough. The urge is simply too strong to sit here and vomit my insides. So I do what I've done—what I've thrived on—for the last six months: I bail. I can't simply kick this habit without some serious help, and although I'm grateful for the time with Chloe, it's just not enough.

Despite her numerous, heart-wrenching pleas, I leave. Out her window, down the lattice, and into the world again. By the time I reach the cottage, it's noon. The sun is reigning overhead. Everybody is on the lake. The boiling heat sits on my tongue, and sweat beads on my brow, but I'm determined. And once I'm determined about something, there's no stopping me.

I only wish I was that way with staying clean.

"It's got to be around here somewhere," I say to myself, thinking. Where did Chloe hide my stuff? How long she was gone determines how far I should go to locate my things. I also need to search for freshly-disturbed soil, where she dug and then repacked the dirt on top of the hole. But in a dense forest such as this, any hope of finding my contents may be a lost cause. This idea sends my phobic brain into a frenzy.

You'll never find your stash, Logan, it tells me. *But she knows where it is. She can tell you. She won't, though, so you're on your own. She won't help you, hasn't yet.*

"Just leave me alone!" I scream, covering my ears with each hand. If I had the ability to wrench this damn voice out, I would. Take a pair of tweezers, maybe some pliers, and pull.

I fall to my hands and knees. *You won't find it.* "Shut up!" It has to be here somewhere. If my mind was functioning correctly, I'd remember the length of time she was away from the cottage so that I could calculate the distance she travelled. But I've never really been fantastic at math. What I do know is that she vanished for a good ten minutes, which means she buried my stuff five minutes out.

She tricked you. She took your things. She's been using them when you're not around. Watch out for her, Logan. She can't be trusted!

"SHUT UPPPPP! Shut up, shut up, shut up! I can't take this anymore. She didn't do anything!"

Behind me, there's a rustle of dirt and grass and twigs. I glance over my shoulder. Chloe stands several feet away, her face creasing at the sight of me. She knows I came looking for the drugs so I won't have to deal with withdrawal. She also knows where the drugs are buried.

Slowly, I stand and turn toward her. "Where are they?" I ask.

Her eyes widen. "Excuse me?"

"You know what I'm talking about. Where are they? Where did you bury them?"

She shakes her head and crosses her arms over her chest. "You know I can't tell you that, Logan. It's for your own good."

"Aaaaghh!" I cry out, fisting my hair. How can she do this to me, when she *knows* I need the drugs back? Does she purposely want to inflict mental pain and suffering?

Yes, says my mind. *Yes, she does. I told you she would, but you didn't listen. You never listen.*

"Stop talking to me!" I shout, but, as usual, my mind doesn't pay attention.

"I'm not saying anything," Chloe says nervously.

She always has something to say. Don't believe a word that comes out of her mouth! It's all a game to her, a trick. And now you're paying for it. How does that make you feel, Logan?

I can't help it: I fall to my knees and beg and wish and pray that my head will stop talking to me, that my stomach will stop churning like the water against the lake's shore, that this gaping emptiness I have inside will be filled with something more substantial than the hell I'm living in.

Chloe's arms encircle my crumpled body, my *failing* body. Because that's what's happening, isn't it? My body is failing me. I'm failing myself. I'm a failure.

"It's okay, Logan. We're going to get through this," she murmurs, each word sending faint puffs of air against my ear, causing my body to shiver. She hugs me tighter and runs her fingers through my choppy hair; I sheared most of the ends last month, when I found a pair of scissors in a trash bin outside one of the souvenir shops.

"I don't want to feel like this anymore," I say, voice splintering.

"Why don't you come back with me? I can make you some chicken noodle soup. That always makes me feel better when I'm sick."

Yeah, but you've never been physically and *mentally sick. The first, maybe, but definitely not the latter. Chicken noodle soup isn't going to help.*

"I think I'll stay here for a little while," I tell her. "Until I feel well enough to walk again."

"Want me to stay with you?"

"No," I say a little too quickly. "No, um, I just want to be alone right now."

The distrustful gleam in Chloe's eyes tells me everything I need to know without a single word: she's fearful for my future, for the monster I've become, and she doesn't want me searching for the drugs, or using again. But, without a word, she stands up, brushes off her knees, and leaves in the opposite direction— where I should be going.

I lay on my side for what feels like hours. The sun descends beyond the horizon, and the stars glitter in all their brilliance. During this time, not a single thought passes through my psyche. I'm void. Blank. Emotionless. I care nothing about past, present, or future. I care about nothing at all. My eyes are totally consumed by the stars, and, eventually, the moon.

Is this what it's always like during withdrawal, the feeling of drifting along, never really sure of where one's going? I don't want to feel like this. I want to be happy and healthy and living a normal life again. In my dreams, I enjoy life with my friends at school, and the football team, of course. My family. Lucas. All of these things mattered to me once upon a time, and they still do. But I don't know if I'll ever really get them back . . .

Sitting up, I stare into the shadows for mere moments before realizing I'm zoning out. I'm in a haze, and I don't know how to shake it off.

"Logan, why won't you get better and come home?" Lucas's voice perforates the night.

"Lucas? Luke, where are you?" I squint and glance all around, but see nothing. And he doesn't answer me. "Where are you?" I call out. "Luke? Lucas!"

For hours, I sit in the same spot, hoping Lucas will make his presence known. Sometime during the latter half of those hours, I realize how fucking insane I've become: I expect my little brother to just pop out of the bushes like he's been hiding there all along. Stupid.

I was also stupid to send Chloe off the way I did. She'd still be here right now, if I had said yes to her staying. But no, I just had to have some alone time.

I stand up, stretching my muscles. I don't know if the delusions and nausea were a part of the withdrawal process, but I hope I won't experience them again anytime soon. Especially not in front of Chloe; that was pretty damn embarrassing.

What I'm most worried about is how long the withdrawal process lasts. What if I have another episode where I wander off into the woods and hear my younger brother speak to me? What if I become so dizzy I can't stand, which causes the queasy feeling in my stomach to turn over and over? What if I'm one big, heaping pile of useless shit after the drugs wear off? I understand they'll fade out at some point, sure. But I'm scared how I'll react once they do.

I don't even know if I remember what I was like before; the old me, who I was. Most of my memories are hazy fragments. Bits and pieces scattered like wreckage of a sunken ship. Now all I have is the new me, still a part of the old, but not exactly the same. I've matured a little, became more of a man. I've learned how to step up in certain situations, but I still have a long way to go.

I meander over to the lake's edge, squatting down and dipping my hand into the cool water. After splashing it all over my face and using it to swish out my mouth, I feel more rejuvenated.

If there's one thing I've learned today, it's that I need to take charge of my life. If I'm ever going to see Lucas or Chloe or my parents ever again, I can't be what they think I am. I have to be *me*. I have to go after what *I* want; otherwise, what am I living for?

Twelve • Chloe

A *clink* on the windowpane wakes me. At first, I think I might've dreamt it happening, but the same sound hits the glass once more. I sit up. Shoving the covers off and still half-asleep, I stumble toward the window. Emphasized only by the pale moonlight is Logan.

I flip the latch and stick my head out, hissing through gritted teeth, "What are you doing here?"

"I wanted to know if you'd give me one more shot." He shrugs. "If you don't, that's cool. I wouldn't blame you."

With a sigh, I motion for him to climb up.

"Let's talk," says Logan, as he enters my room. Typically,

these aren't words anybody wants to hear, but this is Logan we're talking about. He's bound to have some excuse.

"Okaaay," I say, plopping down on my bed, not giving him my full attention. "So talk."

"I'm sorry for what I did earlier. I should've let you stay, and I shouldn't have taken my anger out on you."

I nod curtly. "Thanks."

"I just . . . I feel like I'm losing my mind, and I don't know how to stop this reaction."

I finally glance at him. "It's called withdrawal, Logan. From what little I know, it sucks. You're sick and your body is pissed because you've starved it from the one thing it's hungry for. If you can get over this mountain, then you can conquer anything. But this," I continue, "this is the hardest part. Just stay with me, okay? It's crucial that I don't lose you to heroin."

He hangs his head. "You won't lose me, Chloe. Not now. Not ever. I've made stupid mistakes and I'm ready to man up to them. For you, for my family. For *me*."

Clutching his hand, I link our fingers together. "I can't keep going back and forth, you know. You're a good person, but you're right: you've made some terrible mistakes. You have to decide if being clean is really worth it. If not, then I can't help you anymore than I already have."

"I'm ready," he says with confidence. "I can't watch my life just pass me by, never fully able to rein it in."

"I understand."

He squeezes my hand. "All right. So, what's the next step?"

"How about we rest up before we create another checkmark on the to-do list?"

Kicking off his shoes and losing his shirt, he scoots backward on my bed, pulling me with him. I lay with my back to his chest. His arm is coiled so tightly around my waist, I can't move even if I try.

Logan leans forward a little, his lips grazing the edge of my ear, and says, "Good night."

I shiver, and he presses me closer to him, if that's even possible. "Night," I respond.

~~~

"Why don't we grab something to eat? My treat," I say as Logan exits the bathroom. Steam follows him out.

While he was taking a shower, I thought about how he probably doesn't remember the last time he had a hot meal. Sandwiches are becoming repetitive in the Sullivan household, and I think it's time for Logan to bulk up. Right now, he's just lean muscle.

"Have you ever been to Bernie's?" he asks.

I brighten. "It's only one of my favorite places to eat!" But that was when my family was still a family, and we used to participate in family-like activities, such as eating meals together. I haven't been to Bernie's since our summer vacation last year.

Logan gently rests his hand on my thigh, the heat of his palm sending goosebumps up my leg. "What's wrong?"

I shake off the thought of *before*. Before my family was a wreck. Before I met Logan. I also shake off the sensation he gives me as his fingers firmly squeeze. "Nothing. I just haven't been there in a while. But it's cool; Bernie's is fine with me." I smile so he won't be confused by my abnormal behavior.

"Okay. Bernie's it is." He grins, and we have an unspoken moment, where our eyes hold each other's glance longer than normal. "Chloe . . ."

"Yes?" I peep.

He breaks the connection by looking away and removing his hand from my thigh; there's an instant chill once it's gone, despite the mild room temperature. "Um, I just wanted to say thank you for helping me. Nobody in this world has the patience or time to help. Not one on one, at least. So, uh," he says, clearing his throat, "thanks."

"Yeah, well, it was either help you or watch Lifetime movies and reality TV shows with my mom all summer." I lift my hands in the air, weighing the options like an ancient scale, and settle on Logan having the upper hand. "Mmm. You won."

"You mean, you missed all kinds of awesome TV for me? Aww, how sweet."

I snort. "I'm not entirely sure about the awesome part, but yes, I missed it all for you. Plus, my mom likes to hit the bottle while lounging. Well, who am I kidding? She hits the bottle all the time, and, with her on anti-depressants, it's not fun. Although, she's slacked off on the drinking lately. Maybe she's finally coming to her senses." I shrug. "Who knows?"

"Damn," says Logan. "So, you basically have to babysit her?"

"Sometimes. But only if she's had a really bad day. I blame my dad, though. She wasn't like this until he started staying late at work and wouldn't return her phone calls. I think she knew then that he was sleeping with someone else." The overheard telephone conversation at the beginning of this summer brushes against my mind, but I quickly push it away. Mom hasn't mentioned where Dad went, but I wonder if he's staying with *her*. Oksana. I doubt Mom knows the new girl's name.

"My parents went through a rough time like that once," Logan says openly.

"What happened?"

"Dad began flirting with this girl at work. I didn't know about it until I stopped by his office and noticed they made a lot of eye contact with each other. I shrugged it off, thinking they were just being friendly, but a few weeks later, Dad's phone dinged while he was in the shower. Mom happened to be in the bedroom at the time, cleaning, and she checked his phone without thinking anything about it. Turns out, it was a text from that girl; she wanted to know if they were still on for drinks later. Mom confronted Dad about it, but he lied and said it was a company get-together, that everybody was going out for drinks, so it was

106

no biggie. I heard the convo when I passed by their bedroom. Later, after Dad left, I told Mom about stopping by his office a few weeks before, how he and that girl exchanged a lot of smirks and glances." Logan rolls his eyes. "Mom told me to watch Lucas, and she grabbed her car keys and practically flew out the front door. I don't know what happened after that, but, as far as I know, Dad and that girl were alone. It wasn't a company thing like he said."

"Oh, my God. That's awful."

"Yeah, they went to marriage counseling for months, and were finally able to work out their problems. Dad complained Mom didn't love him like she used to, and Mom said he wouldn't pay attention to her, or listen when she wanted to talk. I guess it's all about communication."

Too bad my parents can't attend marriage counseling and work out their problems. That'd be a fiasco. I picture Dad complaining about Mom drinking while on prescription meds, and Mom complaining about his affair. Or is it *affairs*?

"But they're okay now?" I inquire.

"Oh, yeah. They sorted through their problems, and they agreed to be more open about what's bothering them. It's worked so far."

"Well, that's good."

"Who knows, maybe your parents could do the same." His mouth curves into an altruistic smile. I know he has good intentions, but he doesn't really know the extent of what I've lived with for the past six months: the constant bickering, the distrust, pieces of small furniture flung across rooms and smashed against walls.

"I don't think so," I say, returning the same empathetic grin.

He slides one arm around my shoulders and crushes me against his chest. "Don't worry about it, then. Whatever decision your parents make, it doesn't mean they stopped loving you, and it sure as hell doesn't mean it's your fault." He releases his grip. "Okay, now, go get ready. I'll head over to Bernie's and grab us a booth, all right?"

"Sounds great."

He practically pushes me off the bed and toward the bathroom.

"I'm going. I'm going." I chuckle, heading straight for my closet to find something to wear.

Logan lifts my window, but not before looking back at me. "See ya in a bit," he says, with a wink.

I giggle like I'm ten years old. "Bye."

He shakes his head and has the biggest, cheesiest grin attached to his face.

After taking a shower and primping myself, I head downstairs. Just as my foot reaches the bottom step, the front door opens and Mom enters.

"Oh, hey, honey. Mind helping me?" she asks.

Damn it. I can't say no because she'll guess something's going on. Saying yes means I'm delayed from seeing Logan any longer. I settle on saying, "Maybe."

"Great." She actually looks better than she has in a while; there aren't gloomy circles under her eyes, she curled her blonde hair, and—*oh, my God!*—is that makeup? I feel bad for advising Logan she's basically a drunken pill-head, because the mother I see before me is the mother I remember from when I was a kid, even as early as one year ago. My happy mother. "Why are you looking at me like that?" she asks, breaking my train of thought.

"Oh, I was just . . . um . . ." I firmly press my lips together. Yeah, I've got nothing.

Mom laughs, and the sound is light, airy, like birds singing in the treetops on a bright, spring morning. She's back. My mom is back!

"You look . . . different," I say.

Her eyebrows shoot up. "Different?"

"In a good way."

She doesn't seem convinced, but if the wry smile at the crook of her mouth means anything, she takes my compliment to heart. "Flattery doesn't imply you can evade hauling in groceries, you know."

I snort. "Of course not."

"But nice try," she says as she passes by me on her way to the front door.

I reach out and touch her arm. "Mom?"

She stops, staring at my hand and then at me. "Yes?"

"I meant what I said about you looking better. I'm glad you

aren't just sitting around."

Her blue eyes search mine for this new, unknown form of emotional expression, one which she and I haven't experienced together in quite some time. "Well, in that case, thank you."

I smile and leave her standing on the foyer as I head outside. The back hatch on the RAV4 is open, and the rear is full of sacks taut with produce and canned goods. Normally, Mom only buys sandwich and junk food. Never before has pasta or fresh veggies been on the menu.

When Mom returns to help with the rest of the fare, I wave my hand over the groceries and ask, "What's all this?" There's enough food in here to feed us for weeks.

"You'll see."

Oh, I don't like the sound of that.

With the last of the grocery bags set on the counter and the RAV4 locked up, Mom and I begin sorting through what needs to be placed in the fridge and the cabinets.

"So . . ." I begin, pressing for a sign she'll explain what the food is for.

She twirls around to face me. "Dinner. Every night from now on. No excuses."

Shit. I'm supposed to be on my way to meet Logan right now and, instead, I'll be dining in. With my mom. What is this world coming to? I think Hell has officially frozen over.

"Um, actually," I start, glancing away so I won't see the hurt in her eyes, "I was planning to go to Bernie's tonight."

110

"Sweetie, if you wanted to go, you should've just told me. We could've gone. I don't want you going out by yourself with that killer still on the loose."

"No, I meant—" But I stop myself, because if she finds out what my original intentions are, there will be another murder in Sandy Shores. "Fine. Let's go." At least Logan will see us, and see why I was sidetracked.

By the time we drive to Bernie's, find a parking spot, and are seated at a table, over forty-five minutes has passed since we unloaded groceries. My eyes discretely scan the restaurant. I'm at an advantage; we're seated at the bar because Mom wants a drink—surprise!—so I can see the entire place.

And Logan is nowhere in sight. Which worries me. The police still haven't found Jake's killer, and I have a gut feeling Logan knows who did it. He won't flat-out tell me he knows, but he won't look me in the eyes the few times I've asked him. And he fidgets. That's a definite sign, right?

So, what if Logan was jumped by the killer? If whoever murdered Jake was blatant enough to leave his body in a parking lot, then why not be obvious during daylight hours, too? I have this crazy idea that Logan is linked to the person who stabbed his friend, and, whoever they are, they might be after him, too.

Thirteen • Logan

It's now been over an hour since I left Chloe's room and she hasn't shown up. What does that mean? Did she purposely refuse to come because, deep down, she wants nothing to do with me?

For the fifth time, Heather, the waitress, stops by my table. "Nothing yet?" she asks, noting the empty seat across from me.

"Fuck this," I mumble to myself, standing up and leaving Heather behind.

"Sir?" she calls behind me. I honestly didn't want to alarm her, but shit, I just wasted an hour of my life and hers. An hour she could've had someone else sitting there, eating, ready to give her a tip soon. Instead, she got me, a loser guy who was *supposedly* meeting someone. Now I just look like a dumbass.

Oh, Chloe, Chloe, Chloe. What am I going to do with you? Do you really want to help me, or is this all just a pity party?

I want to fight against my conscience, but after the way I acted toward her the other day, part of me seriously doubts whether she'll continue to fight for me, the *recovered* me. Even though I still have a long ways to go in that department, I'm slowly getting there. I was a fool to run off like that and search for my drugs—drugs I told her to hide. Then, I had to shrug her off, basically telling her to get lost, after she took the time to search for me.

If this is her approach toward quitting, I don't blame her; I've been a selfish asshole all along, and she doesn't deserve my antics. She doesn't deserve any of me.

I pass through the alleyway beside Bernie's, strutting toward the rear parking lot—the last resting place of Jake. I glance up at the clear, blue sky, as if he might be hovering somewhere up there, watching. I hope not. I hope he's moved on to bigger and better things.

"Rest in peace, buddy," I say, stopping long enough to stare at the yellow tape sectioning off the crime scene. The horrible memory of his dead body, stabbed and bleeding, will stay with me forever. And God knows I should've come forward, I should've told the police I had a general idea of who did this so his family would've had some closure. But I didn't. I'm a coward. Had that been me—and it very well may be by the time all is said and done—I think Jake would've told the cops he knew who my killer was.

"You did this to him," says an all-too-familiar voice from the alley.

Big P's voice.

I turn to run off the opposite way, but stop short of Ice and B. A third, scrawnier man steps forward, too. I've never seen him before.

Big P laughs, and the others follow his lead, like puppets. "Not this time, Logan. I've given you plenty of warning, but you avoided me at all costs." He points toward the scene of the crime and says, "See what happens when I don't get what I want?"

"You didn't have to do that to him. He didn't deserve it. This is between you and me," I tell him.

Big P's face is wiped clean of sarcasm, and he takes a few steps forward. "Listen here, you little shit. Anybody who lies to me is as good as dead. This kid knew where you were and he wouldn't tell us, so guess what? He paid the price. Now it's your turn." With a simple nod of his head to B, Ice, and the new guy, my body is restrained. Big P is so close I can smell his nasty breath. He glares, but I don't break eye contact with him. Then, he hauls off and punches me. My jaw crunches from the impact, and my head twists to the side. I spit out blood.

It takes me a moment to regain my senses, as they've been knocked out completely. "You hit like a pussy," I say with a smile that stings, blood dripping from one corner of my mouth.

I encounter another punch from the opposite side, harder than before. Nobody's lying when they talk about seeing stars, because I'm definitely experiencing those bright, tiny dots right now. Plus, there's darkness around my vision. This time, I'm not so quick to recover.

"What, no more smartass comments?" he jests. "That's too bad, because I think I just figured out a way to shut you up." He pummels me again and again and again. I can't even stand on my own anymore. My head hangs, and there are so many blood splatters on the concrete. Then, with an enthusiastic laugh, he kicks me in the stomach. *Hard.* I wheeze and cough up more blood. I think, if I vomit right now, it'll be nothing but warm, red fluid.

But he doesn't stop there. Oh, no. This is Big P we're talking about here. He's known around the drug community as being one of the most notorious leaders around, and for his bad temper. Because when he's pissed, he's going to take it out on whoever stands in his way.

I just *had* to buy drugs from him. I'm a fucking idiot.

Big P pulls out a knife from his pocket. "Do you know what this is for, Logan?" He waves it around my face for good measure. I shake my head in response. "I'm going to fillet you from head to toe, and then I'm going to dice you into little pieces and bury your remains where nobody will *ever* find them. Do you understand?"

He'll fucking doing it, too, and I have no way to stop him.

"Yep," I choke out.

"Take him," says Big P, with a nod of his head to his boys. They drag me across the parking lot. I steal a glance over my shoulder and see a black SUV parked at the curb.

Well, I think, *this is it, then. This is the end of me. I should've stayed in the damn restaurant.*

I peer up at the sky again, because this may be the last time I see it. Silently, I plea, *Jake, if you can hear me, buddy, show me a sign. I'll make everything right by telling the police the truth. Promise.*

The back door to Bernie's swings open; it's some guy carrying out the trash. He's an older man, maybe in his late fifties, early sixties—the kind that looks like he retired from the military, with faded-green tattoos on his forearms. Definitely not someone I picture taking out garbage.

Look at me, look at me, look at me, I will him in my mind. *FUCKING LOOK AT ME!*

He looks at me.

Stops.

Squints.

Then: "Hey! HEY! What the hell do you guys think you're doing?"

Big P and the rest hurry toward the waiting SUV. The trash guy steps inside the back door and then back out, holding a shotgun. He fires it once into the air, which freezes Big P, Ice, B, and the other guy in their tracks.

"I asked you what the hell you think you're doing!" he yells. As he nears us, I get a better look at him. He's the one and only Bernie.

"Hey, man. We weren't causing any trouble," says Big P. "Best put that away before someone gets hurt."

Bernie looks at Big P and his thugs, and then faces me. I can almost see him taking mental notes of my condition, which, judging by the expression on his face, isn't good.

"Let him go," says Bernie.

"Listen, man, this is none of—"

"I said, LET HIM GO!" He points the shotgun in Big P's face. Big P throws his hands up, surrendering. For now.

Ice and B release their firm grasp on me, but the other guy doesn't. Big P notices. He glares at the dude and says, "Smooth, man, are you deaf?" Finally, Smooth lets go, but not before shoving me toward Bernie.

I stumble to the ground, aching all over, especially my face. I regain my footing long enough to hobble off in the opposite direction, back to the alleyway of Bernie's. I have no idea where I'm going, but it's not safe to be here right now.

Squealing tires shriek behind me, and I know Big P and his boys are gone. I breathe a sigh of relief. "I owe you one, Jake," I mumble. "I owe you big time."

"Hey, kid! Hey, wait!" Bernie jogs in my direction. "Come inside and I'll get you cleaned up. Do I need to call an ambulance for you?"

"Nah. I'm fine." I spew out a stream of blood.

"Son, you obviously haven't seen your face. I'm telling you, you need someone to look at those cuts and gashes. I have a first-aid kit inside. It'll only take a minute." He sounds convincing, and I know he has the right intentions, but I just don't want the authorities involved yet. If he means what he says, though, then I'll take him up on his offer.

Bernie sits me down in his office, in the back area of the restaurant, tucked away from prying eyes. True to his word, he fetches a first-aid kit and begins cleaning me up. Moments of silence stretch out between us, until he finally speaks.

"Did you know those guys?"

"Yeah."

He stops cleaning one wound and looks at me. "Well, you're definitely not friends with them."

I repress a laugh. "No. Definitely not."

"My guess is you got in with the wrong crowd, maybe owe them some money."

Is this guy psychic or what? "I'd say that's pretty damn accurate."

He grunts. "Figures. Kids like you throw their whole lives away on drugs, alcohol, and sex. There's an entirely new world out there for you, kid, and it doesn't involve any of the above for entertainment."

After applying the finishing touches to my open cuts, he hands me an ice pack, which I press against my jaw. "I'm just trying to get my life straight, man."

"Well, you can't do that as long as you hang out with the likes of those boys," he states.

"I know."

He stands up, hands on hips, and assesses his work. "Looks better than before, but it's still nasty. Keep ice on your face to reduce the swelling, and take a few ibuprofens to ease the pain. Tomorrow's gonna be a bitch for you."

Every day is a bitch for me, I want to tell him, but I don't.

Fourteen • Chloe

I stand by my window after Mom and I return from Bernie's. The air cools my skin, and the view from up here isn't all that bad. Crickets chirp loudly, frogs croak by the lake, and the summer nights have a spicy scent to them, like Mother Nature herself has sprayed the atmosphere with a sensual perfume.

A twig snaps, and I jerk my head toward the direction of the sound. Out of the shadows hobbles a figure. When the moonlight frames his body, I know exactly who it is.

"Where have you—" I start, but then I see his face. Dark blue and purple splotches cover his eyes and jaw line, and his eyes are swollen so much, they're almost shut. "Are you okay?"

Motioning for him to climb up so we can talk, he ascends the lattice and slides through my window. Before I can open my mouth to ask what's happened, he crushes me against the wall, his lips finding mine in the dark. He tastes like salt and blood, but there's also a sweetness that follows. Both of his hands grab my face, as if he's afraid I'll pull away. As if he wants to siphon the very air from my lungs because it's what he needs to survive, because the atmosphere around us is too electrically charged to breathe normally. Roughly, his tongue invades my mouth, which is completely exhilarating. Without slowing the pace, I circle his tongue with mine. The constant giving and taking is making me lightheaded. One of his arms loops around my waist, pulling me closer to his body. Unpredictably, I moan, sending him into another round of intense kisses.

Eventually, I pull away, barely able to tell him to stop. It's not that I really want him to; it's just that I don't think I can take anymore. This feeling, like I'm floating atop water, is completely new to me. Foreign. Scary. Uncontrollable. Definitely not the same as the make-out sessions with Jeremy Frazier two years ago, behind the school. Actually, this is *nothing* like that.

Logan firmly plants his hands on either side of my face. He kisses my forehead once, lips lingering, and then says, "Please don't give up on me. *Please.*"

"I won't," I whisper.

"Promise me, no matter what happens, you won't leave me."

I can't exactly promise that. I mean, what if I'm unable to be by his side for some unforeseen reason? "Logan, I don't think—"

"Please, please, please, Chloe," he whispers against my cheek, his breath as soft as a breeze from a hummingbird's wing. He trails kisses down my neck and over my breastbone, completely disorienting me. Then, his mouth dips even lower. I gasp, because I've forgotten I'm only in a slinky, spaghetti-strap top, and boy shorts. He hooks one finger underneath a strap and slowly guides it off my shoulder. I don't protest because, deep down, I don't want him to stop. I want to know what it feels like to have a boy worship every inch of my body. But then there's that nagging bitch of a conscience, and she wants to impede my better judgment.

"Tell me to stop," he murmurs. "Tell me to end it all right now and I will." He lightly brushes a finger over the edge of my top, catching the lacy border and dragging it down, down, down, until he fully exposes me on one side. My chest heaves up and down with each new breath. Thank God it's dark in here; my cheeks feel like they're on fire. He repeats the same, slow motion of revealing the other breast. I yelp when his light stubble scrapes across the underside and all around the center. "Hush," he murmurs against my extended peak. His lips are so close they brush the tip.

I whimper. *Do it already! Put your lips on it and—*

"Relax," he says. "You're too tense. Don't be scared, Chloe. I won't do anything you don't want me to. Understand?" He massages the muscles around my neck, my arms, my waist, my thighs and calves. Slowly, I unwind. "Now, where were we? Oh, I remember." With that, he feasts on my breast. I wish I was joking about this, but I'm not. He literally takes one in his mouth, half devouring it, and sucks. *Hard.* Just like I wanted. All the while, he takes the other taut nipple between his fingers, pinching, rolling, teasing. His free hand presses against my back so that I can't move.

I throw my head back against the wall. *Ohhh mannn.* So this is what it feels like. It's no wonder why women and men can become addicted. This might be better than kissing. I let a moan slip past my lips, but Logan's quick to cover my mouth with his own. "Hush, baby," he says in between kisses. "You don't want your mom hearing us, do you?" Without waiting for a response, Logan invades my mouth with his tongue, exploring as deep as he can go.

My lips feel like they're bruised. My mouth is being stretched to its limits. But I don't regret any of this as Logan carries me to the bed, my legs wrapped tightly around his waist.

He sets me down on the mattress and lies on top of my body, covering nearly every inch. "I don't want to rush things, especially if we won't see each other for who knows how long." With a sweep of his finger over my cheek, he adds, "You're so beautiful. I don't want to ruin you, Chloe. I want everything to be *right*. And if that means waiting, I think we should."

What? "What?"

"We shouldn't do this right now. I'm in pain, and I think we

123

should hold off."

Why does this feel like he just slapped me across my face *and* kicked me in the stomach at the same time? I've heard so many excuses before and none of them hurt as much as his. Although he's supposedly looking out for me, this is as close to rejection as it gets. Which sucks.

I sit up and fix my clothing so I'm covered again. Clearing my throat, I say, "Um, yeah, sure."

"Are you mad? Please don't be mad at me."

He has the nerve to ask me this question after he just told me he doesn't want to be with me? He started it, but he's acting like it's all one-sided. That's it! No more.

"Yeah, actually, I am mad," I say, bolting up from my bed to get away from him. "You can't just lead me on like this. Do you realize how many times I've tried saving you already? And each time, all you do is push me away. After what you did yesterday in the woods, and then not even meeting me at the restaurant today, I don't know if you'll get better or not, Logan."

He reaches for me, but I dodge his hand. "Look," he says, deflated, "I'm sorry. I *was* at the restaurant, and I wish I had stayed." He pauses to shake his head, like he's discarding an unwanted memory. "I can't explain what it's like. I feel crazy. I mean, I was in the woods yesterday, listening to my little brother talk to me, so I must be insane, right?"

"Logan—"

He raises one hand. "Just hear me out, okay? You have no

idea what it's like being so addicted to something, it leaves you breathless. One minute it's there, the next it's not. It's like a physical ache gushing through my blood, as if every piece of me is in pain."

"Actually, I do know what that's like," I murmur.

He goes on, ignoring me. "Not to mention my stomach hurts from vomiting, I'm delusional, I have murderous drug dealers after me—"

"Wait—what?" I blurt. "Murderous drug dealers?" Then it hits me. I cross my arms. I *knew* something like this would happen; Logan wasn't giving me the full story. Ever since he told me about his friend, I felt like something was *off* with his version of the events. Now I know why. "Your friend—Jake, was it?—he was killed by them, wasn't he? They were after you, they knew you two were friends, and Jake somehow got in the way."

Logan inhales sharply, shaking his head, and looks at the floor.

And if they did that horrific crime to Jake, what will they do to Logan? Is that what happened to his face—they got a hold of him? *Oh, shit.*

"You were running from them all along, weren't you? What do they want? Logan, you have to do some—"

"I know what I need to do, damn it! I just don't have a way of getting it. And things are only going to get worse if I don't play by their rules."

Pacing across my room, I realize I can't even wrap my head

around this mess. Logan's in some dire shit right now and there's absolutely no way I can help him. Blood-thirsty drug dealers? Not my thing.

I stop pacing long enough to say, "They want money, don't they? That's what all drug dealers want. How much do you owe them?"

He waits so long to reply that I begin to doubt whether he'll respond at all. Finally, he lifts his head and looks at me. "Five thousand."

"Five—" I can't even finish. Resting my hands atop my head, I bite my lip and stare at the ceiling. How the hell is he supposed to obtain such a large sum of money? I sure as heck don't have it, and I know he doesn't, either.

"Chloe, I danced with death today," he says. "I was seconds away from being tortured mercilessly and cut up into tiny pieces."

"What?"

"Lucky for me," he goes on, "Bernie happened to be taking out the trash. He saw us, grabbed his shotgun, and advanced on Big P and his boys before they hauled me off to Godknowswhere. If Bernie hadn't appeared when he did, I have no doubts that I'd be long gone by now."

"This is fucking crazy," I murmur, on the brink of tears. For him, and for both our sakes. If they find out, somehow, that I'm involved and helping Logan, I'm done for, too.

"Yeah, no shit. Bernie cleaned me up as best he could, but

it'll take some time for me to heal."

"Let me see." I flip on the bedroom light and huff when I see his face. "Oh. My. God."

"That bad, huh?"

"Have you not seen yourself?" I point toward the bathroom. "Go look in the mirror."

Slowly, he stands, and I follow. Turning on the vanity lights over the sink, Logan just stares at himself for the longest time. I don't know the thoughts going through his head, but I can only guess they're occupied with awful memories. Memories of his beating. Ideas of what might've been had Bernie not saved him.

"What are you going to do?" I ask. My voice sounds so small, as if it, too, is afraid of speaking up.

"First, I need to heal and get myself cleaned up. Then, I need to come clean to the police about Jake's murder. And, lastly, there's only one place left I can go to for help."

"Where's that?"

Still staring at himself in the mirror, he tells his reflection, "Home."

Fifteen • Chloe

For the past week, I've done nothing but take care of Logan. His bruises have all but faded, and the swelling in his face is completely minimized. Gradually, he's overcome shivers and nausea, until they are nothing more than a recollection. Today, he's decided to pay a visit to his parents' house, even though he's not sure if they'll still be there, or if they've moved on. I hope, for his sake, they still reside in the only house Logan's ever known.

The problem, however, with visiting Logan's parents is that they live in the next town over, which will take *way* too long to reach by foot, especially in the heat, so I have to convince my mom to either let me borrow the RAV4 or steal it. I don't want to be labeled a criminal, but this is mine and Logan's last resort for help. If his parents don't have the five thousand dollars Logan owes to Big P, then we're royally screwed.

We mutually agreed that I'll drive the RAV4 a couple of blocks up the street, where Logan will be waiting for me. He'll give me directions to his parents' house from there.

"Mom, can I borrow the car for a bit?" I ask as I bound down the stairs. "Just for a bit; I won't be long."

She turns halfway around on the couch and looks at me. "What for?"

I shrug. "I wanted to go for a drive. I'm starting to get a little bored, I think."

"Chloe, come here." She picks up the remote from the coffee table and mutes the TV. "There's something I want to talk to you about."

Oh, God. This can't be good. I drop onto the recliner and wait.

"I talked to your father last night. The divorce papers will be filed as soon as we return home. But, in the meantime, I've thought about where we should live. Now, I know it would be hard on you, since you'll be starting college soon, but I think a move will be best. That is, unless you want to live with your father." She pauses long enough to catch her breath.

"So just buy a new house and I can continue with my life like none of this ever happened," I say.

She closes her eyes and massages the bridge of her nose. "Chloe . . . I don't want to live in Cherryview Falls anymore. I grew up there, and I have so many wonderful memories of that town, but . . ."

She's delaying. God, why is she delaying? "But what?" I push.

"I think now's the time to move on with my life. And if you want to join me, I would love that. If not, then I understand. Your life, your friends, everything you know is back in Cherryview. But this new life? It could be our little adventure." Her eyes are so big and round and hopeful. She wants me to say yes because she doesn't want to be alone anymore. I get that. What I don't get is why she won't tell me where we're moving.

"Mom, I can't agree to anything if you don't tell me where it is we're going."

She tugs at her bottom lip with her teeth for a second or two, then releases. "See, that's the thing. I haven't really decided yet, but there is one place I've always wanted to live."

"And that is . . .?"

"California," she says.

Cali? She has *got* to be kidding me! That's across the country! How the hell am I supposed to visit friends if I live thousands of miles away? And . . . and . . . *oh, my God!* How will I see Logan?

I almost explode into a fountain of tears on the spot. Logan's been right all along: we probably won't see each other again.

This will be our last summer together.

"Just . . . think about it, all right? I don't want you to feel like you have to make the decision now, and I definitely don't want you to feel pressured into choosing between your father and me."

I roll my eyes. "Mom, please. You know I'd choose you over him any day. But don't you think California's a bit of a stretch? I mean, that's a giant leap for both of us."

Please, please, please be joking.

A lighthearted smile curves from ear to ear across her face, and, for a split second, I expect her to tell me it's one big farce. "It is a major change, I know. It'll take us a while to get use to the idea of living a world apart from everything and everyone we knew, but I think it's for the best."

How can she say that? Has she lost her marbles? I mean, it might be great for her if she didn't have me in tow, but why can't this wait until I decide where to go to college? Then, I can move away and live in dorms. She can go eat avocado sandwiches and slurp fruit smoothies on a beach in California, while I stay behind with what few friends I have.

And the Logan thing? Everyone says long-distance relationships never work out. The thought of losing him, of never seeing him again, shatters my heart into itty bitty pieces.

"I just . . . I need some time to think," I tell her, which is true.

She stands up when I do. "Here, take my keys. If you need to ride around and think about your decision, that's fine. Just don't be out too late. And wear your seatbelt." Surprisingly, she follows through with her word, lifting the keys out of her purse and handing them over. I must be stunned because she laughs and grabs my chin with her other hand. "My dear, sweet Chloe, don't view me like I've lost my mind; I already feel like that most days." When I don't respond, her face turns serious. "I trust you, sweetie. Here, take them," she says, grabbing my hand and dropping the keys onto my open palm.

"It's that simple?" I eye her suspiciously, like she might birth a second head from the base of her neck. "Why didn't you let me borrow the car before?"

She glides back to her usual end of the couch and picks at the fabric on the armrest. "Your father never thought it was a good idea. He was too controlling, I guess. But," she says, pausing to take a deep breath, "I want to start fresh, do things my way. I want to learn how to trust others, even when they don't deserve to be trusted. I want to fall in love all over again, with someone who is worthy of my love and who will give me all of theirs in return." She looks at me, then, and I see the sadness and hurt in her eyes. But I'm proud of her for taking risks; most people refuse to because they're afraid they won't succeed. "I just want good in my life again, Chloe. I want to be happy."

I can't stop the tears from rolling down my cheeks. "Oh, Mom." I take a few steps forward, falling to my knees in front of her, and lay my head in her lap. She immediately strokes my hair like she did when I was a child. "We all want happiness," I say, sniffling. "Finding it is half the battle."

"I've found it with you," she says, "so I guess I'm already halfway there."

This only makes me cry harder. I wish I would've spent the past few weeks with her. I wish I told her everything about Logan. But I still have no idea how she'll react, knowing I've been harboring a fugitive drug user. So I don't say anything at all. Not yet, but soon, I'll tell her everything.

I dry my eyes as I lift my head from her lap. "I'll be back later, okay?" One sniffle escapes me.

Mom smiles and whispers, "Okay. Not too late, though."

With my purse and keys in hand, I don't postpone this chance. Plus, Logan's depending on me to get him from Point "A" to Point "B." If I can't drive us to his parents' house, he'll walk. I won't, but he will. He needs the money badly enough, and he needs to see his family again—especially Lucas. I just don't want him on the streets alone, not after what happened a week ago. Next time—if there is a next time—will be worse.

Backing out of the gravel driveway, there are no signs of life on our deserted road. Most of the small-town happenings occur in the "downtown" area, which includes Bernie's, the tourist shops, the Grab-N-Go, and a gas station. This time of day, everyone's on the lake. I mean, that's kind of the point of Sandy Shores, right? To get away from it all; city life, work life, life itself.

As we planned, Logan patiently waits a couple of blocks away. He opens the passenger door and slides in. "Let's get the hell outta here," he says, grinning.

I smile back, ignoring the tightening in my stomach as I think about what life will be like without Logan. *What's he going to say when I tell him that he was right all along?* He made me promise I'd never leave him. And now, knowing what I know, I have to sever my promise and any feelings I have toward him. It won't be easy, but in the end, it'll be worth it. For both our hearts.

"Where to?" I ask.

"Anywhere but here," he teases. Then: "Take Main Street past Bernie's and out of Sandy Shores. Once we hit the main road, it'll be a little while, but I'll show you where to turn." He glances over at me and rests his hand on my thigh.

Oh, jeez. Talk about not being able to keep my focus. I'm almost delirious from his touch. We haven't kissed since *that* night, and neither of us has spoken about what went down. It's as if it never happened. But I'm okay with that. Why? Because I'll have to drop the bomb on him soon about moving to California.

Lightly squeezing my thigh, Logan says, "Ease up, babe. You can't choke the life out of the steering wheel; it's already dead, you know." He chuckles at his own joke.

I don't bother looking at him. This is too much. I hate keeping secrets. I hate that I didn't tell him as soon as he got in the vehicle that I'm moving. I hate that his hand is on my thigh, even though he doesn't want to have sex with me. I want to scream, "*Stop leading me on!*" but that won't get me anywhere. If anything, it'll make me look like one of those clingy girlf—

I stop myself. I'm not his girlfriend. I'm a girl who gave him the time of day when he was down on his luck. I'm just a girl who wanted to escape the constant bickering of her parents and used Logan as a pet project to keep my mind off the problems at home. We're nothing, really. This thought, coupled with the fact that there is no future between us, nearly rips a gaping hole in my stomach. Literally, I bend forward at the wheel.

"You okay?" Logan leans toward the dashboard so he can look me in the eyes.

"I'm fine," I say, waving him off. "Just feel a little nauseous."

"We can pull over for a second, if you want," he says.

"No. I'm fine. I swear."

Get a hold of yourself, Chloe! God, I just want to scream and cry and drop him off at his parents' house without looking back. Maybe that's what I should do. Make it nice and easy for the both of us. He'll have his old life back, and I can start my new one. In a way, we'll both get what we wanted. Him: to be with his family and friends again. Me: to get away from my parents fighting.

I feel like I'm at standing at the shores of the sea as a storm rages overhead. The water performs the commands of the storm, and I'm at the mercy of the water. Yet this doesn't hinder the storm from ordering the water to swallow me whole. As I stand near the beach, a one-hundred-foot-high wave looms over me, like it's deciding whether I'm even worth its effort. Eventually, it consumes me, and I drown.

"Chloe, stop the car," says Logan.

I pull off on the side of the road, far enough that the traffic behind me doesn't have any trouble passing by. It's then I realize that my face is wet.

"Baby," Logan coos, "what's wrong?"

"Don't call me that," I say through clenched teeth. More tears spill out and down my cheeks.

"What?"

I close my eyes. *Give me strength.* "I'm not yours to call 'baby' so I'd appreciate it if you'd stop calling me that."

Sarcastically, Logan says, "Um, okaaay . . ." Like I'm the crazy one who has issues.

I check my side mirrors before tearing off the shoulder, tires squealing, leaving a trail of black, burnt-rubber smoke behind.

"What the fuck is wrong with you?" Logan asks. "You're kinda scaring the shit outta me."

"I just . . . have a lot on my mind, okay? I promise to get you to your parents' house in one piece." At least that's a promise I can keep.

With a heavy, extended sigh, Logan finishes giving me directions to his home. We don't exchange any additional words for the remainder of the way. Not until Logan instructs me to turn on his road.

As I slowly creep up the street, Logan leans forward, squinting his eyes. "Yep, they're still there. The truck's outside, and so is Mom's car."

Glancing in the same direction, I notice the only house with a car and truck parked on the paved driveway. The house is a modest, two-story structure, with a coffee-colored paint job and bright pink, orange, and yellow flowers under the two front windows. It's one of those cookie-cutter homes, the ones people buy so they can live the American dream and feel like they're in a safe neighborhood.

I pull the RAV4 to a stop on the curb. Logan nearly leaps out of the passenger seat, but I can't say I blame him; he's been caged up with a crazy, emotional girl. But more than that, I think he's just really excited to see his parents after six long months.

"C'mon," he says, gesturing for me to get out.

I shake my head. "I don't think so, Logan."

He jerks back, like I smacked him. "What? Don't be silly. I'm sure they'll love to—"

"Logan, honey? Is that you?" A middle-aged woman steps out of the front door with a shocked expression, like she can't believe her son has returned. Like she thought she'd never see him again. Her shoulder-length, brown hair flutters with the summer breeze, as does the knee-length dress she wears.

"Hey, Mom," says Logan. "I've, uh . . ."—he clears his throat—"I've missed you."

She squeals. "Oh, my dear, sweet boy." They close the distance between them and embrace in a long, bittersweet hug. His mom strokes his hair, and I can't be sure, but I swear, even from this distance, I see tears slide down her cheeks. She murmurs more words to him. I can't hear what she's saying, but I'm sure her words are filled with love. "Logan, who is that with you?"

He collects himself, like he almost forgot I'm here. "Oh, Mom, this is Chloe. She's helped me get clean. Chloe, this is my mom, Marcie."

"Nice to meet you," I say.

"You too, dear." She smiles. "Why don't you two come inside and drink some of this lemonade I just prepared?"

Logan glances back at me. "Chloe, you coming?"

"Oh, I don't think—"

Frowning, Logan cuts me off. "Don't be like that. C'mon."

So much for bailing and forgetting any of this ever happened. I lock up the RAV4 and trudge in behind Logan and Marcie. The inside of the house is decorated in the same tan colors as the paint on the outside, with the exception of black accessories—candle holders, bookshelves, and even the dining room table. Marcie has lit a couple of candles, and the aroma creates a calming atmosphere. Which is exactly what Logan needs right now, if he's going to discuss borrowing five thousand dollars.

"Where's Dad and Luke?" Logan asks as he and I sit down in the living room.

Marcie busies herself with fixing us lemonade. "Lucas had practice. Sally took him and her boys, so I didn't have to go. He should be home soon. And your father will be home anytime now from work. They had him pulling overtime again. He's been doing that a lot lately. Here you are," she says, handing me a cold glass. She gives the other glass to Logan, who sits on the couch across from me, and then sits down beside him. "So, Chloe, tell me a little bit about yourself."

Well, I definitely didn't come here to be interviewed. "Um, well, I'm from Cherryview Falls, three hours north of here. I was an honor student in high school—I just graduated in May—and on the track team, and I'm a total movie nerd. I haven't decided where I'll attend college yet, but I have a few applications filled out." I shrug. "That's about it, I guess."

"Uh-huh. I see." Is that a disapproving look that crosses her face? Like I'm the most boring person on the planet, so what am I doing with her son? Interesting. "And how did you meet Logan?"

Logan nearly chokes on his drink, but I continue. "I found him in an old, abandoned cottage by the lake. I felt bad for him, and I couldn't just leave him there."

"He must've needed your help quite badly," she says. "He wouldn't let us help him for months."

"Mom!"

She sighs. "Logan, honey, it's the truth. Your father and I love you dearly, but you are as stubborn as they come." She turns her attention toward me again. "We offered to send him to a wonderful rehabilitation program, but he refused. When there were no other options, his father kicked him out. It was the

139

saddest day of my life."

"I ran into Charlie," Logan says. "He said you went looking for me that night."

Marcie nods. "I stayed out for hours, but I couldn't find you."

"I'm not one hundred percent better, Mom, but I'm trying."

She wraps one arm around Logan's shoulders. "It's all that we ask for. At least you can say you tried. If this doesn't work out—"

"It'll work out this time. I promise."

Marcie contemplates this for a moment, then says, "Okay, baby. I believe you." Abruptly, she stands up. "I've got to make a couple of phone calls, but I'll be back shortly. There are some chocolate chip cookies on the bar in the kitchen, if either of you want any." With that, she walks down the hallway, to the back end of the house. I assume she's calling Logan's dad, maybe even her friend who took Lucas to practice, to let them know Logan's home.

"Are you nervous?" I ask him, noticing his leg bouncing up and down.

"A little."

"Don't be," I say. "I'm sure they'll be happy to get you out of this mess once and for all."

Marcie returns a little while later, looking refreshed. "Your father is on his way home, and Lucas should be here soon. Sally's pulling the boys out of practice early. He doesn't know yet that you're here."

"He's in for a big surprise," says Logan.

Logan, Marcie, and I chat about what our summer has been like, how the heat is unbearable this season, and how Logan's family has been getting by without him present. I think it's good for Logan to hear that his family is still hurting with him gone; it lets him know he's needed. All this time, I've pinned them for the type of people who don't care what happens to their family, who take advantage of how good life is. But I was wrong. It's blatantly obvious that Marcie cares very much for the well-being of her children, and she and Logan's dad have been concerned from the start.

A young boy, who I can only assume is Lucas, walks through the front door. Sally and her boys aren't far behind him.

"Hey, Mom, I'm home!" Lucas yells. He sees me and stops. "Who are you?"

"I'm Chloe."

"Oh. Are you my mom's friend?"

"No, I'm Logan's friend."

His eyes light up at the mention of his brother. "Logan?"

I nod.

As soon as he enters the living room and sees Logan, he freezes. He takes in the sight of his long-lost brother, like this is all a dream. A very real dream. "Logan!" he shrieks, running over to his older brother with outstretched arms. Logan picks him up and swings him around and around, like he weighs nothing at all.

"I missed you, Luke. I missed you so much." Logan sets Lucas down, but Lucas won't let go. His arms remain circled around Logan's waist. He buries his face in Logan's shirt, maybe embarrassed that we see him crying. Logan bends over and whispers in Lucas's ear. Lucas nods.

"It's good to see you again, Logan," says Sally.

"Oh, thank you, Mrs. Hardy."

"We should have a barbeque at my house this weekend. There's plenty of room for the boys to play," she says.

Marcie nods her head in agreement. "That's sounds lovely. I'll be in touch. And, Sally, thank you again."

Sally smiles at Marcie, Logan and Lucas, and then at me before she grabs her boys and leaves.

Lucas sits down next to Logan on the couch, snuggling up against his brother. Marcie sits on the other side, wiping the tears from her eyes, and wraps her arms around both of her boys. I feel like an outsider, watching this small family reunited. But then I pinch myself, because I helped. I did this. I brought Logan here.

A smile of satisfaction curves my lips. Never in my life have I felt as accomplished as I do now. It's a good sentiment.

The doorbell rings, breaking us out of our pensive trances. Marcie stands up and fixes her hair, then strides to the foyer. On the other side of the door is a girl, about my age, with long, black hair, tanned skin, and the brightest aqua-colored eyes I've ever seen. Marcie welcomes her inside and leads her to the living room. The girl eyes me for a moment, but then her focus is intent on Logan, who looks like he's seen a ghost.

"What are you doing here?" he asks.

"Hey, Logan. I've missed you." She waits, and then adds, "We've all missed you."

Seconds roll by, and the room is so tense I can puncture the air with a knife.

"That still doesn't answer my question," he says. "What are you doing here?"

"Logan," Marcie pipes up, "is that any way to act towards Audrey? I thought things were good between you two."

Say what? Okay, so my gut is right: they have a past. Or *had* a past, I should say. I haven't seen this girl patrolling the streets of Sandy Shores, searching for him.

"We were good, once upon a time, and then she dumped me right after you guys kicked me out."

Audrey rolls her eyes and plops down in the recliner next to the couch. "Oh, please. I never broke up with you. You were the one who pushed me away because you thought I couldn't handle your addiction. But we *never* broke up."

Why do I have the feeling that last part was directed at me? If what she says is true, this means Logan has had a girlfriend the entire time we've been together. It means we never really meant a thing; we were a lie.

Suddenly, I'm suffocating. The weight of the room literally feels like it's crashing down on my chest. The walls are closing in. I can't breathe. Oh, God help me, I can't breathe.

"So," I begin, catching what little air I can, "you're his girlfriend?"

Audrey gives me a smug look. "Don't tell me you actually fell for him. He's very convincing with his hugs and kisses and empty, broken promises. He always has been. And trust me—if there's anyone who knows this, it's me. But yes, for the record, I am his girlfriend."

I catch the last bit as I exit through the front door, somehow making it to the sidewalk before I throw up.

Sixteen • Logan

"Chloe! Chloe, stop!" She's not listening to me, though. Through a fit of tears, she runs around to the driver's side and jumps in. Tires squeal as she takes off down the road and out of sight. I just stand there, dumbfounded, wishing she would've believed me over Audrey, wishing she would've at least *listened* to what I had to say.

Audrey and I haven't been together for six months now. I don't care what she says. The girl broke up with me because she couldn't handle my addiction problems. Never once did I see her looking for me. If anything, the bitch was probably spreading rumors and lies about how I overdosed and died, left her for another girl, or ran away from everyone and everything this town had to offer. Why can't anyone just tell the truth these days?

"That's too bad," Audrey says behind me. "I hope you didn't actually have feelings for her."

I whip around to face her, trying to keep my rage in check. "First of all, you are *not* my fucking girlfriend. And even if you were, you're a shitty one. How many times did you look for me, Audrey?" I might as well have slapped her, but her expression morphs back into her typical, sour face. "Tell me how many!"

She chews on her bottom lip. "Well, there was this one time I thought about—"

"You *thought* about it, but you never actually went through with the idea, did you?" I snort. "Like I said, *shitty* girlfriend. Not that you were ever a good one, anyway. You sucked at keeping our private life private, you sucked at kissing, you sucked in bed, and you sucked because you made me feel like a piece of shit in front of all our friends. You were always picking on me, embarrassing me—and for what? To make you look and feel better? Chloe isn't any of those things; she's twice the person you'll ever be."

Audrey rolls her eyes. "Whatever, Logan. You're just pissed because I ruined what little affection there was between you two, if there was any. She looked like one of those brainiacs who only care about homework, and who stay in on weekends because they don't have any friends. *Please.* You could do *so* much better."

"Chloe is better. Better than you, better than anyone I've

met. She may keep her nose stuck in books, but at least that means she's smarter than you'll ever be. At least that means she'll get somewhere in life and won't rely on her daddy's money." I glare at her.

"Oh, whatever! I won't rely on my dad's money my entire life. In case you were wondering—"

"I'm not."

"—I have a few colleges lined up in the fall. Harvard, Yale, Dartmouth. You get the idea. I bet your precious Chloe won't ever get into any place that nice, will she?" She smiles, and it sends a chill down my spine.

"Oh, please. The *only* reason you're getting into any of those places is because your dad is rich and made a large donation to one of the three. My guess is Harvard, since that's where he graduated from." She opens her mouth to interrupt, but I cut her off. "And if you tell me I'm wrong, that means you've probably slept around with some of the head honchos just so you could get on a list, which doesn't guarantee you'll get in. So, if the former is true, that means you'll still be depending on your dad's money for years to come. If the latter is true, that means you're more of a slut than I thought you were."

Leaving Audrey standing in the driveway with a dropped jaw, I stomp inside, slamming the front door behind me and locking it.

"And you!" I shout, pointing at my mom. "Why the hell did you call Audrey to come over?"

Mom gasps and quickly covers Lucas's ears. "Logan, please control your language around Lucas." She removes her hands. "Lucas, honey, why don't you go play in your room for a bit? I need to talk to your brother."

Lucas's eyes dart between Mom and me, but he never says anything, dutifully walking upstairs to his bedroom.

Mom turns to me. "Logan, I didn't know. I honestly thought you two were still together. Audrey asked me several times if I had heard anything from you. She even came over after you . . . after you were . . . gone."

I exhale loudly, rubbing my face and combing my fingers through my hair. "I have to go to her, Mom. Even if she never wants to see me again, I have to tell her the truth."

Mom nods a few times, then says, "Take my keys and drive carefully." She motions toward the small table by the front door, where a bowl filled with car keys, loose change, and peppermints rests. "I'll notify your father. Don't leave us waiting this time, Logan. We're all ecstatic to see you again."

"I won't."

She quickly hugs me before I dart out the front door. Thank God Audrey took the hint and left. I hope I never have to see her again. What she did to Chloe is unacceptable, and I hope I can alter Chloe's opinion of me before it's too late.

It's amazing how, when you're with someone, the world seems right. The stars align, or whatever. But if you make one small mistake, they never forget. They lug your problems around,

148

rubbing them in your face when necessary—whenever they want to hurt you and cause major damage. That's not love. Love is more than just a pretty face with a nice personality. Love is knowing your significant other's heart for what it is, both good and bad, and seeing what they're worth. When they have problems, you don't drag them through the mud and muck; you help them to their feet and walk beside them every step of the way.

That's what Chloe did for me. So, is that love? I don't know, but I intend to find out. My heart beats rapidly every time I think about her. Is that love? I still adore the way she scrunches her nose without thinking; it makes her look years younger. Cuter, even. Is that love? She's polite and selfless and the most beautiful person I know inside and out. I can't stop thinking about her. I want to be with her every second of every day, and my heart literally aches when we're not together. Is that love? Probably.

"Ugh, Chloe. What have you done to me?" I say aloud in the car. It'll be another thirty minutes or so before I reach Chloe's house, and even then, I don't know that she'll be there.

But I have an idea where she might be.

~~~

I park along the curb of Chloe's street exactly thirty-three minutes later. No way did she run inside, crying for her mom to see. My theory? She's at the cottage, or somewhere by the lake near the cottage.

It takes me some time to find her, and it definitely wasn't an easy search. She was *in* the water, swimming. I stand at the shore and shout, "Come talk to me!" She pretends like she didn't hear as she floats atop the water, arms outstretched. "Don't make me come out there," I warn. Reluctantly, she stops floating and swims toward shore.

As soon as her foot touches land, I reach out, but she sidesteps me and wiggles away from my grasp.

"Just . . . listen to me, Chloe," I say. "Audrey lied to you. She and I aren't together."

Chloe doesn't respond as she tugs on her dry clothes.

"Okay, so, you're pissed," I continue. "I get it. I'd be pissed, too. But you have to believe me. I wouldn't do this to you."

She finishes buttoning her shirt, slips her feet into her flip-flops, and walks back toward her house.

"Chloe, please talk to me. Say something. Anything. Tell me I'm a lazy, good-for-nothing bastard who has shitty priorities." I catch up to her, but she won't look me in the eyes. I've never felt so invisible in my life. "I'm sorry, okay? But I'm hurt, too."

She stops, frowns, and then asks, "Why?"

"Because you believe Audrey over me, which means you don't trust me."

She sighs and rolls her eyes dramatically. "It doesn't mean that I don't trust you, but it's a little too obvious that you two still have feelings for each other. I should've paid attention to the signs, anyway." She resumes walking.

"What *signs*? I swear to God there's nothing between her and me."

"Oh, please." She huffs. "The sexual tension I felt between you two in the span of five minutes is more than anything I've felt between us."

I grab her shoulder, forcing her to stop walking. "Is that what this is about? Because I have a sexual past with Audrey and haven't done anything with you?"

"No, it's not like—"

I back away, running my fingers through my hair, laughing at the sky. "Oh, my God."

"Logan, I swear that's not what I—"

"Then, enlighten me, because that's exactly what it sounds like."

She inhales and exhales slowly. "Okay. So . . . I just meant that there was something stronger between you two, stronger than what you and I have, so when she said you guys were still together, I panicked because I could *feel* she wasn't lying. She truly believed you two were a couple. And since you two already had a past, it might be easier to revert to your old ways."

"Let me get this straight," I say. "You think just because she and I dated, I'll go running back when she calls?"

Chloe hesitates, shifting weight to her right leg, then answers, "Maybe."

"That's the most ridiculous thing I've ever heard. I'm not her

151

little bitch—I'm not anybody's little bitch—and I sure as hell won't be going back to her. She treated me like shit, and I was tired of it."

"I don't know, Logan . . . You can stand here and say these nice things and make up stories, but the truth is you went running when heroin called. So, how is that any different than Audrey?"

Without a response, I just stand there like an idiot. Like she just slapped my brain out of my skull and I can't think. I watch her turn and stroll off, and yet I don't do anything. *Go after her, Logan! Go!* My legs aren't listening to my head, though. *Make her believe you!*

Finally, my mind connects with my legs. "Chloe, wait." She doesn't listen, so I yell, "WAIT!"

Now she stops. Turning around, she looks annoyed. "Make it quick."

I amble over to where she stands. "Just tell me what you want," I whisper. "I've stopped using. I've tried working things out with my parents. I'm not dating Audrey, or anyone else. I don't know what else I can do to make you happy." Reaching out, I grasp her by the shoulders, forcing her to look me in the eyes. *Say something—say* anything—*damn it.* I can't stand to see her like this.

She shrugs out of my grip. "All I want is for you to get your life back on track. I want you to be happy."

"Done. See? Not so bad."

Shaking her head, she articulates, "That's not what I meant,

Logan, and you know it."

I snort. "Whatever. I'm fine."

"Are you?" Her delicate features crease in so many different places. "I think, if you had the chance, you'd pick up the habit again."

WHAT? "Wow. Way to have some fucking faith in me." She moves to touch my arms, but I step backward a few feet, out of reach.

She licks her lips nervously. "Just . . . hear me out, okay? The truth is that I care a lot about you, but I don't completely trust those feelings, or you—not yet, anyway, but I'm trying."

"Want to know what I think?" Her baby blues stare up at me; anticipation and worry perform the tango in their depths. "I think you started this by throwing a pity party. 'Oh, God, the poor, homeless boy with a horrible life. I must help him.' But that quickly turned into some fucked-up feelings, and then you realized that if you help me, if they help me"—I gesture wildly to the millions of random people surrounding us in the world—"if *anyone* helps me, it would be a good thing . . . for me. But for you? That's a totally different story. Because the truth is you have a fucked-up life like me, you *see* yourself in me, and you can't fix your own problems, so you're trying to fix mine."

She opens her mouth to speak, but closes it just as fast.

"But who's going to be the one to help you, Chloe?" I reach out to cup her face in my hands, my thumb gently sweeping over her bottom lip. "Nobody, then?" She shakes her head. "So I guess that leaves me."

She nods and sniffs. "I guess."

"I'll take care of you, baby. It might be a while, but I will."

"You can't," she murmurs, on the verge of tears.

"Why not?" I lift her chin, forcing her to look me in the eyes. "Tell me."

She just shakes her head, unable to reply.

"Well, since we're getting things off our chests," I say, "now might be a good time to tell you that I'm fucking crazy about you. There was never a point in my life where I cared so much about anything—not football, not my home life, none of it. I've never met anyone who has a heart like yours; you're so willing to give it all away to those who need it most, even if it means losing some of the pieces forever. You're the most infuriating, selfless, beautiful person I've ever known, and I thank the universe every day that I met you."

Damn. For real, I think I'm gonna vomit.

"You're absolutely terrified that when I get better, I'll move back in with my family and we'll never see each other again," I say, my chest expanding and contracting to compensate for intense breathing.

She tears up. "Yes, I'm terrified I'll never see you again."

I can't help the grin sliding across my face. "Oh, Chloe, what am I going to do with you?" I lean down and kiss her lips. She doesn't hesitate to smash her body against mine, squeezing me tighter and tighter. I lock my hands in place at her lower back.

With my mouth pressed against hers, I hoarsely whisper, "It's not going to happen, you know. You and I will pull through our issues, separately and together, understand?"

She clings to my gaze. "I don't know if we will, though. That's what I'm afraid of."

"What do you mean?"

Biting her lip, she falters.

"*What* do you mean?" I repeat, my voice rising.

One tear escapes and slides down her face. "Mom and Dad are getting a divorce, and Mom is moving out of state. She wants me to go with her. When I got back from your parents' house, I told her my decision."

What the fu— No. Just no. I shake my head. *Calm down, Logan, just calm the fuck down.* I grapple for some sense of the situation. Maybe it's just one state away, or maybe it's one of the other states along the East Coast. That won't be so bad, right?

"Where?" She just stares at me, so I ask her again. "*Where* are you moving to, Chloe?"

Her bottom lip quivers as her eyes drop to her feet. "Logan, I think it's best—"

"DAMN IT, TELL ME!"

"California, Logan," she says, raising her eyes to meet mine. "We're moving to California, the state where dreams are either made or destroyed. I don't know which it'll be for us."

I jerk away from her as if she slapped me. Cali? The opposite side of the United States? I pace a few yards away, grasping

155

sections of my hair and pulling. Maybe the pain will wake me up, because I *have* to be hallucinating. But Chloe still stands in the same position, her cheeks now displaying a fresh coat of tears. *"How the hell are we supposed to see each other if you move out there?"* I can't quite force the words to roll off my tongue, but I know she's thinking the same.

"Logan, please . . . don't make this h-harder than it already is," she chokes out.

I stop pacing to ask, "How long have you known?"

"She told me before we left earlier. I knew she'd move out, but I didn't know where to. And I can't stay with my Dad." *You know, for obvious reasons,* is what she's basically telling me.

I can't be pissed at her; it's not her fault. But shit, this is Cali we're talking about here. I don't have the money, or a job to produce the money, so I can move out there with her.

"We'll figure this out," I say, gathering her in my arms again. Resting my head atop hers, I plant several kisses on her wet hair. "We'll get through this. Do you trust me?"

She sniffles. "Yes."

"Okay, then. I have to get back to my parents and Lucas. I have to talk to them about borrowing the money so I won't have Big P on my trail forever. Do you want to come with me?"

She nods. "Let me get a shower first."

"'Kay." I grab her hand as we meander back to her cottage. The sun pokes through the leaves from the canopy of trees above us, and all is calm on the lake. If this were any other time, I'd say it was a perfect day to be outside. But with Big P and his boys after me, being in the open isn't an option.

Chloe enters through the back door, and I climb up the lattice—our usual routine. Less than a minute passes before she opens the window to her bedroom.

"I won't be long," she says.

I clear my throat. "Aren't you forgetting something?" I can't keep the lame grin off my face as I slide through the window and close it behind me.

Her eyes widen. "What?"

I motion with a finger at her attire. "Strip."

"Logan, I don't—"

Shaking my head, I interject, "Strip. You owe me one, remember?" All joking aside, and with the smirk wiped from my face, I add, "I want to see you."

Chloe stands there, probably weighing her options, but, ever so slowly, she begins unbuttoning her shirt. I park my ass on the edge of her bed, toss my backpack on the floor, and then scoot backward so I'm sitting against her wall. She loses her shirt and unzips her shorts. Standing in nothing but her bra and panties, I notice she doesn't seem nervous. Like, she *wants* to put on a show for me. My smirk returns, as do the naughty images she normally inserts in my mind. Reaching around her back, she unclasps her bra, letting the straps gradually slide down her arms. She pauses for a dramatic effect, then lets her bra fall to the floor. I gulp. *Gorgeous* is the first word to pop in my head. *Fucking beautiful* are the next two when she slithers out of her panties and stands before me completely naked. God help me.

"Now can I take my shower?" She raises one eyebrow and a wicked grin forms on the curves of her lips.

"I . . . um . . . yeah, sure"—I swallow hard—"I guess."

She giggles. "I don't think I've ever seen you speechless."

I growl. "I'm two seconds away from stripping down and joining you."

She narrows her eyes and saunters toward me. "Did you just growl?"

"Chloe . . . I'm warning you . . . Don't. No, stop." I throw my hands up so she won't come any closer. I'm about to file a missing brain report with the police. 1-800-HAVEYOUSEENLOGAN'SMIND. Because I've seriously lost it. Somewhere.

She presses her stomach against my outstretched hands, and I reluctantly let her move forward. More. More. More. Until she straddles me. My dick is rock hard, straining against my zipper. All it'll take is one tug to set it free.

I summon what little self-control I have left to tell her, "Not now, Chloe. God, I want to, but not like this."

She leans forward and whispers against my ear, "No excuses this time."

Battling with myself over whether I can do this right now, I remember there are several condoms in my backpack. *Don't do it, Logan!* says one side of my conscience. The other is screaming, *Yes, yes, YES! Now's your chance!* By the end of the summer, she and I may not be as close as we are now. We won't even live in the same state. The thought of losing her, of maybe never seeing her again, rips my heart from its strings. If this is what it takes to keep her, then so be it.

"Yeah, fuck the excuses," I say, and claim her mouth harder than I've ever kissed anyone, because I want her more than I've ever wanted anyone. Her perfectly-shaped tits are so close to my face, I can't help but pull away from her lips so I can suck on them. Chloe throws her head back and moans. "Like that, baby?" I ask before I take her other peaked nipple in my mouth.

"Yes," she barely murmurs. Her mouth forms a perfect "O" and her eyes are already half-lidded.

"And my guess is," I say, pulling back to watch her next reaction, "you can feel everything here." I press my middle finger against her clit, rubbing it around in circles. Her mouth opens wider, and her eyes fully close. No sound emits from her throat, except harsh breaths.

"Yes," she whispers. "Ooooh. Don't stop, Logan. *Please.*"

"Begging me, Chloe?" I lean forward and, before I take one of her rosy peaks in my mouth again, say, "Beg *harder.*"

She cries out as I quicken my pace, matching the rhythm between my sucking and my circling her swollen bead. With my free hand, I keep her steadied by pressing it against her lower back. Her body begins to bounce up and down, and I grunt at the thought of her doing the same to my dick. Right now, it's raging to be set loose; so much so, it aches.

Instead of finishing her off, I roll her over so she's underneath me. She's in the sex fog right now, so anything I do to her is dreamlike. Hazy. Fan-fucking-tastic. I trail warm, lingering kisses down the front of her chest, stopping at her bellybutton long enough to jab my tongue in and out a few times. Her thighs tense, and I know I've hit a mark.

"Oh, Logan. *Please.* I need—"

"Ssh, baby. I know. But you asked for this, so guess what? You're going to get it. But I'm going to do it the *right way*. Understand?"

She barely nods her head, still in her sexual euphoria.

I chuckle, but it comes out raspy and hoarse. God, I haven't been this turned on since . . . well, I don't know when. I reach down and carefully unzip my jeans. My dick tumbles out, and I can already feel the pre-come collecting on the tip. Fuck, I'm not going to last long.

My tongue creates languid circles on the inside of Chloe's left thigh. I nip and lick, moving down at a leisurely pace, until I cross her sex, where I stop long enough to breathe warm air and flick my tongue once. Her back arches, and she grabs the comforter with both hands. Pressing on, I slide my tongue over her folds and all the way to her right thigh, continuing the same slow, torturous bites and tongue-thrashings.

"Logan," she exhales in one breath. "Logan, *please.*" She's definitely begging for more, but she doesn't really have a clue what she's begging for just yet.

I smirk. *You want more, Chloe? Wish granted.* I dip my mouth to cover her sex, twirling my tongue around it a few times. Chloe's body tenses, her back curving again. I carefully take her clit in between my front teeth, brushing the tip with my tongue. Over and over and over again. Sliding two fingers inside her, I realize how soaking wet she is—and so tight. Her muscles clamp my fingers, and I can feel the effect all the way to my throbbing member, which now flinches according to the way she moves, as if it can't wait to be where my fingers are.

"Logan, I— Ooooh."

I close my lips around her and suck like it's a straw in my favorite milkshake. All I can see from my point of view is Chloe's arched back, her tits forming perfect hills on a naked plateau. I reach up with my free hand and pinch her left nipple, twisting and rolling it around my fingers. God, her muscles just tightened around my fingers. She's not going to last much longer.

As if on cue, she cups both hands over her mouth and releases a muffled cry, her body shaking uncontrollably in the aftermath. But that doesn't mean I stop. I want her screaming— *pleading*—for me to end the sexual hold I have over her body.

She reaches down and grabs the back of my hair, pulling. The sharp tingle I feel on my scalp only makes me want her more. With her body still convulsing each time I suckle, I know it won't be long before she comes for me again. That's the plan, anyway.

161

I continue my unhurried assault on her sex, lapping it up, changing the pace. My fingers continue to glide in and out of her, and to switch things up, I add a third finger. Every time I drive my fingers inside her, I imagine it's with my own dick, so my hips are pretty much pummeling the mattress of their own accord. Chloe's hips move up and down as she fucks my tongue. I spread her folds apart, so her sex is more sensitive, more exposed. Her breathing matches each thrust of her hips, and I grunt as my hips match hers. If we keep this up, I'm going to come all over her fucking comforter.

"God, I'm going to— Ohhhh."

She arches her back, and the shudders follow. Underneath her hand, her muffled cries cascade to nothing but soft mewling.

I rise up. "Chloe, if you want me to stop now, just say so."

Descending from her high, she elevates herself into a sitting position, eyeing my enlarged shaft. As she licks her lips, I feel my dick respond by bobbing once. "Can I?" she asks. Her eyes are so big and round and innocent, which is funny, considering what we just did was anything but.

"Chloe, I won't last long. It probably wouldn't be—"

"Please, Logan? I want to return the favor," she adds, getting all sheepish on me. She lowers her eyes, and then brings them back up, meeting mine again.

I almost collapse. Who is she, and what has she done with my Chloe? This girl is a vixen, straight-up. To tease me further, she opens her mouth wide, expecting me to just insert myself.

162

"I'm not going to last long, baby," I tell her again.

"But if I get you off now, you'll last longer afterward, right?"

I pause for a few seconds before sighing roughly. "Yes."

She grabs me and slides half of my member in her mouth, moaning. I almost lose my load. Ever so slowly, I begin slipping my dick in and out of her. She uses one hand to hold it in place, and the other reaches around my backside, grabbing my ass and digging her nails in.

"Oh, *Chloe*." I groan and close my eyes.

She pulls me all the way out of her mouth and looks up. "All or nothing, Logan."

"Sweetie, listen. I would, but it'll choke you, and I don't want that to be your first experience."

She rolls her eyes. "I can handle it."

"Whatever you say . . ."

She resumes her previous position, and I slowly slide my shaft in until it hits the back of her throat. She gags. I begin to pick up the pace as Chloe grabs my ass with both hands, her nails digging into my cheeks. Just when I should stop, she urges me to go on by pulling me toward her. I clasp her hair away from her face, and her eyes never leave mine. God, does she know what she's doing to me?

"Chloe, I'm not going to make it." I try tugging her head away, but she won't budge. When my hips stop pumping, she finishes the job by continually moving her mouth. I thrust twice and throw my head back, gritting my teeth. With my legs and body and mind still recovering from what just happened, still feeling like they're tingling all over, she sucks all of me and swallows. I shudder.

Quickly moving to lay her back, I let my weight fully rest on my arms beside her. I lean in for a kiss and grapple with my backpack next to the bed, reaching in and fumbling around. Aha! Found it! I snatch a condom and rip open the wrapper with my teeth.

"This will hurt," I tell her. "But I'll go slowly until the pain eases, okay?"

She nods once.

I roll the condom on. Gently, I press myself to her opening and, inch by inch, slide inside her. She bites her lip and squeezes her eyes shut, like she's in pain. I pull all the way out and then press my way back in. She whimpers.

"Chloe, look at me," I say. I wait until she opens her eyes and stares directly into mine. "Tell me when, baby, and I'll stop."

"No, it's okay. I'm okay. Just . . . keep going."

I don't want to hurt her, but damn this feels so good. In an attempt to ease the pain and get her mind off of it, I bend down and kiss her. She gradually opens her mouth to me, letting me slide my tongue in and around. Her whimpers become soft moans as I continue my slow entrance and exit of her body. As her legs wrap around my waist, her hands find my ass, fingernails digging in.

"I'm going to speed up a little, okay?" I place a lingering kiss on her lips as I up the tempo. Her back arches, and her mouth opens to cry out, but I swiftly cover it with mine again. "Ssh. None of that," I say in between kisses.

Her eyes take on a hazy glaze. "Logan . . . Oh, God . . . Don't stop."

I chuckle, low and hoarsely. "Wouldn't dream of it, baby."

Balancing on one straightened arm, I wrap my other arm underneath her waist and lift her hips. Using her legs as leverage, she matches my thrusts with her own, nearly sending me over the edge. I pump faster—*harder*—and each time, she meets my force with equal vehemence. Our bodies glide against each other, our lips are constantly intermingling. Pressure builds, and we both fall, fall, fall over the precipice of passion. Together. As one.

Lying here, limbs entangled and hearts racing, I nestle my face against her neck and plant delicate kisses on her skin. "Promise me something?"

"Anything," she replies breathlessly.

"Whatever happens, wherever life takes us, we'll always be together."

She turns her head slightly toward me, just enough so she can give me a sidelong glance. "I promise."

I sigh with relief. "I'm going to find a way to be with you in California, even if it takes months, years, or most of my life."

She rests her head against mine.

Taking a deep breath, I say, "Do you ever feel like there's

more than what's around us? I feel like we're not living up to our full potential. Like, there are so many things to do and see in the world, and we haven't even begun to imagine what's in store for our futures."

She smiles. "Is that your new goal in life? To see the world?"

I rise up and look her in the eyes. "Only if you're there to experience it all with me. Maybe we can start a new to-do list."

Her smile fades and is replaced by a serious expression. Tracing her fingers across my cheeks and jaw line, she says, "I'll always be with you, as long as you want me."

"And I'll always want you."

She grins. "Then, it's settled."

We share a laugh.

"Now," I say, "about that shower . . ."

Seventeen • Chloe

I can't say I saw *that* coming. If somebody told me two hours ago that I'd have sex with Logan, I would've laughed in their face. He and I weren't exactly on speaking terms after Audrey showed up, so . . . yeah.

The craziest part is that I can't stop smiling. Like, I'm literally beaming from ear to ear. I have a good feeling about Logan and I being together; we might make it, after all. I was so worried that, once I told him about mine and Mom's move to California, he'd blow me off and forget anything between us ever existed. So I was a little shocked when he seemed distraught by our future cross-country travel. We just have to do this one last thing, and then he and I can start focusing on our future together, which apparently involves seeing the world.

"Mom's probably worried I'll never return," says Logan. After we took a shower together, I fixed my hair and make-up, and we dressed. Now, we're about five minutes away from his home.

"I think she trusts you more than you give her credit for. It may not seem like it, but I saw the love she has for you and Lucas."

Logan squeezes my thigh; his hand has been resting on it for the entire car ride. "Thanks, babe." A minute passes before he speaks again. "I just hope they have dinner cooked."

"Why's that?"

"Because that's the only time I can reason with them. Why are you giggling at me?" He grins as he sneaks a glance in my direction. "I'm serious! They won't listen to me any other time, except at dinner. I know it's weird, but that's my family for ya."

"So, if we walk in and get situated, and they haven't offered dinner, maybe we should suggest it," I say, raising one eyebrow and waiting for him to agree.

Logan nods his head a couple of times and narrows his eyes at the road. "Good idea."

Five minutes later, we park on the curb outside Logan's home. There's a police car parked in lieu of the car we're in, directly beside the truck. Is this about Jake? Did the cops find out about Logan's involvement? This can't be good.

As we enter the house, the man in uniform is speaking to Marcie as Lucas runs wild through the house.

"Logan, you're back!" screams Lucas. He runs directly to Logan and leaps into his arms.

Logan laughs. "Of course I am, buddy."

"Mom said she was afraid you wouldn't return and we'd have to go look for you again," Lucas goes on. "She said she thought you might run off."

"I'm not going anywhere."

Lucas turns to his mom. "See! I told you!"

"Calm down, Luke," says the cop. He seems tired—exhausted, even—as if his lack of sleep is taking its toll on his mind and body. Dark circles stain the skin under his eyes, and he has gray patches of hair on either side of his head, just above his ears.

"Lucas, honey, why don't you go wash up for dinner?" Marcie says, urging Lucas toward the hallway. Lucas takes off, full speed ahead, rounding the corner from the living room and barely stopping long enough to turn into the bathroom.

"Chloe and I were just wondering if you guys would be eating," says Logan.

The police officer stares at me. I feel like he's tacking me to a wooden board with six-inch nails. Why is this so unnerving?

"So you're the Chloe I owe thanks to," says the man. "You look mighty small, young lady, to do such considerable repair on Logan."

Marcie swats his arm. "Oh, Phil, don't scare the poor girl."

He chuckles and extends his hand. "I'm Phil, by the way. Logan's dad."

His dad is a freaking cop? No wonder they kicked him out; it would've looked horrible on his father's reputation as a police officer, not to mention the fact that his dad can't exactly support a drug user when he's out fighting crime every day.

I shake his hand. "Nice to meet you, Mr. Andrews."

He makes a dismissive gesture. "Please, call me Phil. And come on in. Have a seat."

We all sit down; Logan and I on the loveseat, Phil and Marcie on the couch. Seconds tick by without a single word. I wonder if this would've gone better had I not been here, then Logan and his parents could've chatted about whatever family problems they need to work on without feeling awkward.

Marcie clears her throat. "I'll just . . . finish dinner." She goes to the kitchen, which has a small nook for the six-seat dining table, and fishes out the dinnerware.

Phil turns his attention to Logan. "It's good to see you, son."

"Yeah, you too," Logan returns.

"I can't say it hasn't been rough on all of us, but we've gotten through each day, mostly for Luke's sake. He didn't know what really happened. We told him you were visiting family members out west, and that was that."

Logan nods. "It's best he doesn't know. At least, not for a little while, until he's older."

Feeling awkward, I stand up. "I'm going to see if Marcie needs help with anything." Before Logan or Phil can protest, I make a break for it. Marcie finishes laying out the last of the silverware on the table as I arrive. "Can I help with anything?"

"Oh, no, dear. I think I have it all covered."

"Okay," I say, still lingering around. I don't really want to go back to the living room because Logan and Phil are mostly likely having a heart to heart. It's not my place to listen in. It just feels . . . invasive. They might be having a special moment, so who am I to ruin that?

Lucas comes bounding back into the kitchen. "What's for dinner?"

"Chicken pot pie casserole," says Marcie. "It'll be ready in about five minutes. Why don't you sit at the table until it's ready?"

Lucas obediently sits down, facing us. "What are Logan and Dad doing?"

"They're talking, sweetie. They'll join us for dinner when they're through, okay?"

"'Kay."

"Chloe, why don't you have a seat, too?" Marcie says as she wipes off the counter. "By the way, I feel I should apologize for earlier. It wasn't my intent to start drama between you, Logan, and Audrey. I didn't know they weren't . . ." she trails off without looking me in the eyes. *I didn't know they weren't together anymore* is probably what she meant to say. But the way

171

she mentions it, it's as if she never wanted them to break up in the first place.

I just nod and take a seat across from Lucas. He smiles at me, and I smile back.

"You're a lot nicer than Audrey," he whispers.

I lean forward and so does he, like we're sharing our deepest, darkest secrets. "You think so?"

"I know so. She was mean to me. But you seem nice."

Grinning, I add, "That's because I am." I wink at him, which only elongates his smile.

"And I think Logan likes you, too," he says.

"Oh, really?"

"Uh-huh." He bobs his head up and down with each syllable. "Annnd I think you guys should get married."

Whoa, little buddy. "Oh, I don't know about that."

He actually seems offended. "Why not?"

"Well, it's too soon. Maybe if we last a couple of years."

"What are you two whispering about?" Marcie asks, almost causing me to jump out of my skin.

"Nothing, Mom!" says Lucas.

Just as Marcie takes the casserole out of the oven, Logan and Phil walk in, looking as glum as ever. I guess whatever they discussed didn't go so well; the withered expression behind Logan's eyes is enough to make me question whether his parents will help. He softens his expression with a half-smile and sits down next to me, grasping my hand in his.

Logan whispers in my ear, "I told him about Jake."

I shoot him a look. "And?"

"I have to go down to the station first thing tomorrow."

I nod. That's understandable. At least he'll be able to put this behind him once and for all.

Phil sits at the head of the table, while Marcie places a trivet at the center, with the casserole on top.

"Looks good, honey," Phil says, rubbing his hands together.

Marcie adds the final touch—a ladle—to the dish and takes her seat at the opposite end of the table. "Eat up." She grabs Lucas's plate first and scoops a spoonful of the casserole onto it. "Careful, baby, it's hot."

Lucas licks his lips and his eyes grow round. "Mmm!"

She picks up my plate next, then Logan's, and, finally, Phil's. When everyone else is taken care of, she fixes her own plate. We all sit in awkward silence for the first couple of minutes before Lucas takes the plunge.

"Why's everybody so quiet?" he asks.

Gotta love twelve-year-olds.

"Everyone's enjoying their food," says Marcie.

For the entire meal, Phil and Marcie chat about nothing but what their lives have been like since Logan's absence; Phil took on extra hours at the police station, and Marcie is a stay-at-home mom, who manages to find time to create jewelry and sell it online in a craft shop. Lucas has been busy with middle-school baseball, which uses up a lot of Marcie's time by running him

173

and his friends to practice. She and Sally rotate the trips with their boys.

After the table is cleared, and Lucas has taken his shower and gone to bed, Logan and I sit down with Phil and Marcie to discuss why we're really here. I can almost feel Logan's heartbeat hammering through his chest, his palms dewy with sweat. I'm anxious for him. This is big. *Huge.* And if they can't help him, who will?

"I'm not going to bullshit with you guys," says Logan. "I need your help."

Phil leans forward, resting his elbows on his knees, and forms a steeple with his hands above his mouth. "What kind of help?"

Marcie rests her hand on Phil's thigh—a sign of concern, I think—and says, "Logan, honey, you know we'll help you with whatever it is you need, as long as we are going forward. We don't want you to revert to your recent past."

Logan's eyes roll upward. "Mom, *please*. This isn't about me relapsing." He inhales deeply, and, in one gust, says, "I need money so I can pay off my drug dealers."

Phil and Marcie swap a quick glance.

"Honey—" Marcie begins.

"How much?" Phil interrupts.

"Five thousand." Before either one of them can refuse, Logan adds, "I know you two started college funds for Lucas and me. If you want, take it out of mine so it won't make a dent in your pockets."

Phil rubs his forehead, and Marcie looks like Logan just told her he's dying and only has two weeks to live. What would my parents have done if the situation were reversed? Would my mom have given me the same expression, one that's fearful and distressed? Would my dad have said no? Would they both have said no? My gut tightens at the thought of putting my parents in a corner and asking them to make a decision on such short notice. Knowing my dad, though, he would've said something along the lines of, "Just give her the damn money." My mom would've listened, because she always obeyed him, loyal wife that she was. But now that they aren't truly together? I think they'd disagree.

"That's, uh . . . that's a lot, son," says Phil. He stops massaging his brows long enough to stare pointedly at Logan. "What'll happen if you don't give them the money?"

"They'll do to me what they did to Jake—or worse."

Marcie gasps. "That poor boy who was murdered in Sandy Shores?"

"He was one of my friends," Logan says. "He died because of me."

I clasp his arm and rub my thumb over his skin. "You can't blame yourself for what happened to him."

He hangs his head, crushed. "I blame myself every day."

"Son, this wasn't your doing," Phil assures. "What happened to Jake was misfortunate, but you can't blame yourself. This money obviously means a lot to you, so—"

175

"It means everything to me. If I don't get them paid off, they could find out where you guys live. Mom could be home alone with Lucas one day and they'd break in. God, I don't even want to think about it." He closes his eyes and shakes his head, thinking about losing his mom and brother. "The point is," he continues, "I just want to move on with my life, and they're only holding me back. I want to be done with the bad and focus on the good."

"And we'll support you every step of the way," says Marcie.

Phil nods in agreement. "Of course. I'll go to the bank tomorrow—"

"No! I need the money tonight. I want to be done with all of this."

"Okay," Phil says. "I'll just go now, then." He checks his watch. "We only have a thirty-minute window before they close, so I'll see what I can do."

"Thank you," Logan says, his voice nearly a whisper.

Phil grabs his keys from the round bowl by the front door. "Marcie, you coming?"

Marcie replies, "Yes. Let me just get my things." She flurries around the living room and kitchen, picking up her purse, cell phone, and wallet, which was hidden in one of the kitchen drawers.

"We'll be back soon," says Phil, closing the door behind him.

Logan and I sit in the quiet room, fingers entwined, nerve

endings on fire. Before he started the conversation with his parents, I had hoped they'd see his side, and I'm glad they did. I had been worried they wouldn't see clearly, only blinded by key words such as "drugs," "drug dealers," and "five thousand dollars." Now, we have nothing to be anxious about. My stomach can stop flopping over, my palms can stop sweating, and my heart can stop rapidly pounding against my chest. It's over. Well, *almost* over. Logan has to actually get the money to Big P, and then we can be rid of the past, like it was all a bad dream.

As if he can read my thoughts, Logan says, "I'm going to call him. Big P. I'll tell him to meet me tonight." He looks at me, then. "When we wake up together tomorrow morning, it'll be like we started a brand new life."

I don't have the heart to tell him we've pretty much done that already. He changed everything when he decided to stop using drugs and infuse integrity into his life once again. He's made up with his family for good, and he'll be a role model for Lucas.

"Okay," I say, smiling.

Logan fishes an older-model cell phone out of the dish by the front door. He waves it around. "My old cell phone," he says. "I've got Big P's number stored in the contacts."

"Don't forget to block your home phone before you call."

"Our number is private, because of my dad's line of work, and we're unlisted in the white pages. Ah, here it is." He meanders back into the kitchen, picking up the corded phone attached to the wall. As he dials the Big P's number, I sense both his nervousness and relief. Soon, all of this will be behind us. "I've got your money," he says, voice cracking. "Yeah, tonight . . . I'll meet you there." And then he hangs up. "Well, that was easy. Now for the hard part—meeting him face to face."

I just want to kiss him and hug him and tell him everything will work out, because I truly believe it will, but my gut twitches when I think of Logan meeting Big P, alone, at night. After what Big P did to Jake, and the incident at Bernie's, where Logan barely escaped, I won't put it past him to have something up his sleeve. Something disgustingly malicious.

Twenty minutes later, Phil and Marcie return with the money—cash, of all things, which is exactly what Big P wants. I highly doubt drug dealers take personal or cashier's checks.

"It's all here," says Phil, opening a deposit bag full of one-hundred-dollar bills. My eyes bulge. I've never seen so much money in my life! "Do you need me to come with you?" Phil asks.

"No, I've got this, but thanks. I'm just going to run Chloe home, and then I'll meet up with them."

Phil hands over the bag. He and Logan briefly hug, and then Marcie plants a swift, motherly kiss on Logan's cheek.

"Be safe," she says. "I don't want to lose you again."

Her words cause a chill to ripple up my spine.

Eighteen • Chloe

Logan and I pile into his parents' car. Before we get to the end of the street, I say, "I'm not going home, you know. I'm not going to leave you to this by yourself. What if they try something?"

He snorts. "No offense, baby, but how are you going to stop them?" Turning his head toward me, he raises one eyebrow.

I shake my head and pay attention to the houses we pass. "I can't, but I can try. Maybe they won't pull anything if a girl is around. Guys are like that sometimes."

"Chloe," he says, sighing, "these guys don't give a damn. They wouldn't give a damn if their own mothers were with them, I don't think."

Well, *that's* reassuring. "I'm not going home," I reiterate. "I refuse to get out of this car."

"So, you're going to make this hard on me? I'll drag you out of here if I have to."

I snap my head around. "No, you won't."

He chuckles. "You don't think so, huh?"

"I know so. You wouldn't harm me."

A serious expression falls upon his face, like a dark shadow. "No, I wouldn't, and I don't want them to harm you, either."

"Please, Logan? I won't be a bother, but I can have my phone ready, in case something happens. I'll call 9-1-1, or your dad."

"Fine," he says nonchalantly.

"That's it? No fight?"

"No fight, but that's as long as you stay in the car. Understand?"

I nod. "I understand."

Logan veers the car in the opposite direction of Sandy Shores. We follow the main road, pass through neighborhoods, and end up on a different side of town—the rundown side. Buildings are sealed like iron cages, cars are from a separate decade, and nobody strolls along on the sidewalks. It looks like the neighborhood doesn't have the time or funding to maintain the properties, and with all the tourists flocking to Sandy Shores, they're probably hard-pressed for the government to provide spending money. I think every county in America has at least one area like this. My theory? If the community pitched in and worked together to clean up, this would be a cute town, with tiny shops and restaurants.

Turning left at a light, Logan drives us down a side street and over railroad tracks. "Should be up ahead," he says.

The sun sets on the horizon, and the street lights have flickered to life, illuminating the dark road. We drive underneath an overpass with very little traffic, and Logan parks the car to the side, killing the headlights. Both of us get out for a brief moment of fresh air, and I glance around, evaluating the setting and whether or not anyone will hear our cries for help if something goes wrong. Absolutely *nothing* surrounds us, except shrubbery and trees. There's no housing, no pedestrians, nothing. We might as well be in the middle of a desert, with vultures swarming us, eagerly waiting their turn to pluck the flesh from our corpses.

"I don't like this, Logan," I say, crossing my arms. A chill rides up my spine—the same feeling I got when Logan's mom said she didn't want to lose her son again. "Something's not right about this. Something's *off*."

Logan rolls his eyes. "You're over thinking this. I'm pretty sure they won't do anything now that I have their money. It's all about the money, baby."

Even if that's true, I don't believe him. These guys have waited too long to get their money.

"I just don't like this," I say again.

"You don't have to do anything, except sit in the car. I'll

181

hand them the package, and then we can leave." He kisses my hair and squeezes me against his chest. "How does that sound?"

I take a deep breath and exhale. "Sounds good."

"It's times like this when I want H," Logan says, so quietly my brain questions whether he really said it.

Never removing my eyes from his face, I whisper, "You don't mean that."

He frowns. "But I do. When I'm stressed, that's when I miss it the most."

Headlights beam around the corner, blinding us. They quickly shut off, and the black SUV creeps to a halt several yards away. Whoever is driving kills the engine. I hold my breath as all four doors open. *There are four of them, not just Big P.* Usually, Logan only talks about Big P, Ice, and B. That's it. Needless to say, they've added a fourth groupie, another man.

The main guy, the man I'm sure is Big P, flicks two fingers over his shoulder, signaling the others to follow. "I'm surprised you contacted me, Logan, after what we did to your friend. I'm also surprised you weren't smart enough to meet us in a more convenient location, somewhere that has witnesses." His lips pull back in a sneer, and his eyes burnish with delight.

Logan says, "You knew I'd eventually pay you back, but you also knew my situation. How could I have come up with five thousand dollars when I was homeless?"

"Not my problem, kid. You knew what you were getting yourself into when you bought the H from me, and you knew you had to pay interest for every day you were late. That due date came and went, so now you have to pay more."

"More?" Logan looks like Big P just decked him. "I don't have more. I barely got this much."

"Then we'll take care of the problem," Big P says calmly. He snaps his fingers and one of his men stalks in my direction. His biceps are the size of cantaloupes, and there's light perspiration sheen on his bald head. I race around the back of the vehicle and take off running. I hate leaving Logan, but if this means I can escape and get help, then I'll gladly do it. I just hope they don't do some serious damage to him while I'm—

Oomph. I plow into the ground, knocking the air out of my lungs. I'm immediately flipped on my back as the giant laughs maniacally.

"Don't fucking touch her!" screams Logan. Dazed, my head rotates from side to side. I glance over at Logan. Big P's other two men are restraining him, but Logan is still fighting. "Chloe, *run!*" he yells as his eyes connect with mine.

I want to, but I have this big guy lying on top of me, forcing my hands up over my head and pinning them to the ground. *Oh, no.* I begin to kick him off, but he sits on my legs.

"I'm going to have fun with you," he says, grinning. "You're a little spitfire." Then, he leans forward so I smell his acrid breath. I close my eyes and move my head away, but he roughly grabs my chin and jerks it toward him. "And you know what I like to do with fires? Put them out." The last bit is whispered, just

183

for my ears.

I scream, but he hastily covers my open mouth with his, shoving his tongue to the back of my throat. I bite down. *Hard.* The second I taste his blood, I spit it out.

"Bitch!" he roars, freeing one of his hands to slap me across the face. White flecks dance across my vision. When my head rolls around, I search for Logan. He's crumpled on his knees, sobbing.

"That pretty boy of yours ain't gonna do shit," says the monster looming above me.

Focus, Chloe. Focus on getting out of here alive, to save yourself, and Logan.

The more I try to focus, the dreamier this reality becomes. Again, I try to release my legs from this man's weight and kick him, but it doesn't work. So I lay here, mentally and physically preparing myself for the worse.

He rips my shirt down the front, buttons popping off, and pushes the remnants off to my sides, practically drooling when my bra is exposed. With one swift stroke, he tugs my bra down, revealing my breasts. Licking his lips, he dips his head and begins sucking. I cry out, kicking and flailing even more.

"STOOOP!" I shriek, but he bites down, sending a surge of pain through my chest.

"That's for biting my tongue, you fucking bitch. Now, spread your legs for me. I want to make sure your pussy is nice and wet before I ram my cock in you."

My tears are blinding. I can't think straight. Somewhere in my mind, I know I should fight this, but my body is giving up; I'm not strong enough to fight this man off. "Stop! Please, stop!" I screech again.

He laughs as he unbuttons and unzips my shorts. Grabbing hold at the waist, he yanks them down, along with my underwear, far enough that he has a view of everything below my waist. He jams two fingers inside me and wiggles them around. I throw my head back, crying out. But he doesn't stop. He takes my protesting as confirmation to continue his sick game.

"So wet, *baby*," he says excitedly. I pinch my eyes shut and face away.

POP! POP!

Shots ring out in Logan's direction. I scream his name before I analyze the scene. From this point, everything plays out in slow motion. Logan aims a gun at Big P, whose hands are in mid-air as a sign of surrender. Big P's other two men, who were restraining Logan, are lying face down on the pavement, blood pooling around their bodies.

"Don't move," Logan orders Big P. He marches over to where I am, lifts his hand, and points the gun at the beefy guy who just molested me. "She's not your fucking baby," he says, and pulls the trigger. The sound is deafening, and blood sprays my face and body as the man slumps over. I push him off of me as I scurry a few feet away.

I've never seen Logan so, so . . . *lethal*. Pissed isn't the correct term to describe him right now. He's enraged. Obviously willing to murder. And one look at me lying half-naked on the ground, covered in blood, washes away all emotion from his face. He lays the gun down and reaches out, pulling me into his lap. I've never felt so elated in my life, just to know I'm safe in his arms.

"Oh, baby. I'm so sorry," he chokes out. We both cry; for what we just went through, for how close we were to losing each other, for the implications Logan may face once this is all over. "I'm so sorry," Logan repeats again and again. He kisses my forehead, my cheeks, my nose, my chin, and, finally, my lips, even though I'm covered in someone else's blood. "If I could go back and do this all over again, I would. I wouldn't have brought you with me. I just knew this was a bad idea. Can you forgive me?"

"What's there to forgive? It's not your fault," I say, sniffling.

"Are you kidding? All of this is my fault. I never should've picked up drugs in the first place."

Clasping his face with my hands, I tell him, "If you hadn't picked up the habit, we wouldn't be together. It's been an extreme ride, but I've loved every second I've spent with you."

"Promise?"

"I promise."

He wipes away the tears from my cheeks and tenderly kisses me. Pulling back, he says, "C'mon. Let's get out of here. I need to tell my dad what happened." He arranges my clothes into a semblance of order, carefully zipping my shorts and tugging the remaining portion of my shirt over my exposed breasts, which I push back into my bra. "There," he says. "Chloe . . ." He shakes his head, and I know what he's about to say. Another "sorry." Exactly what I don't need. I don't want to be reminded of that man's filthy hands on and inside me; I just want to be cleansed of him and any reminder of his touch.

I press my index finger over Logan's lips to silence him. "No more, okay?"

Over Logan's shoulder, I catch a flicker of movement. Big P reaches toward his back and pulls out a metal object glinting in the light of the street lamps. A gun.

"You're not going anywhere, not after the mess you've made," says Big P.

"Logan!" I scream, but it's too late. Big P fires off two rounds, straight into Logan's back. Logan's body freezes, his eyes bulging from his skull, and then he sputters and falls over. "Logan, baby! LOGAN!" I shake him, but his eyes are dulling out, losing their vivacity.

"Ice may have done a number on you, baby girl, but it's *nothing* compared to what I'm going to do," says Big P.

"Please don't hurt me," I beg.

"You see, Logan's already killed three of my boys, so it's only fitting I do what I want with you and then dump your body where nobody will find it. Maybe the lake. Maybe the ocean. So, if Logan does live through this, and I doubt he will, he'll *never* see you again, just like I'll never see my boys again." He aims the gun at my head.

I grasp Logan's lifeless hand in mine and squeeze. *Stay with me, Logan. Be alive. Don't leave me.*

Tires squeal as three cars tear around the corner, red and blue lights flashing, sirens blaring. All three policemen throw their vehicles into park and use their car doors as barriers between them and Big P.

"Drop your weapon!" one of the officers shouts.

"Drop your weapon and get on the ground!" yells another.

I can see it in Big P's eyes: a look of pure suffering. He *wants* to kill me. He wants to avenge the deaths of his friends, his boys, so he's weighing his decision. The wheels are turning in his mind, and it's almost as if I can hear his thoughts: *I can kill her before they take me, and my boys' murders will be justified, even if that means a longer sentence.*

"Sir, we're not telling you again. Drop your weapon!"

Another one hollers, "Drop it!"

Big P's finger fumbles on the trigger, but, determined, he pulls.

Nineteen • Chloe

It jams.

In moments such as these, it's the minor seconds that count. Seconds that can make or break you. Seconds that can save your life. And, lucky for me, one of the police officers seizes the opportunity, the *second*, to pull his trigger.

It doesn't jam.

Big P stills, and then collapses on the asphalt. All three police officers run to me, one of which is Logan's dad.

"Are you all right? Are you hurt?" Phil asks, squatting down in front of me. "I followed you two after dinner. I just had a bad feeling about all of this." He waves toward the crime scene in front of us.

All I can do is mutter incoherently and bawl my eyes out.

He places a hand on my shoulder. "You're going to be all right, sweetie." He pivots toward his son and presses the radio on his shoulder, mumbling a numeric code. Within minutes, more sirens wail and appear in a show of flashing lights. Paramedics wheel a stretcher to where Logan lies. One of them checks his heart rate, while the other uncovers his fresh wounds. Carefully, they load his unconscious body onto the stretcher and into the back of the ambulance, poking him with an IV and other miscellaneous gadgets.

I watch the ambulance leave with Logan and almost lose my composure. As I stand up, Phil encircles me with one arm, and I sag against him, crying out.

"They're going to take good care of him," he says, his voice catching on a couple of words. "It's all right. He's going to be all right." He hugs me even tighter. "Why don't you come to the station with me? I'll need a recap of the events, in detail. Can you do that? Better yet, can you do it for Logan?"

I nod.

"Okay, let's get you situated, then." He leads me over to his patrol car, and I sit down in the backseat.

During the ride, all I think about is Logan, whether he's going to make it, how we've come this far, and how horrible it'll be if he doesn't pull through. Everything will have been in vain. Phil is quiet, mostly. Is he thinking about Logan as much as I am? He has to be. If I were in his place, I'd be rehashing if there was anything I could've done differently.

Phil parks in front of a square, brick building, where, directly in front of us, the police department logo and name are proudly displayed on a rectangular sign. "Chloe, you don't have to do this right now, you know. You can wait, if it's too painful."

I sniffle. "Doesn't matter if I do it now or five years from now; it's something that'll never leave my mind. So, let's get this over with."

Phil nods his head once in understanding, but doesn't say anything. Irritably, I wipe the tears from my cheeks before I exit the car, before anybody sees me as an awful mess. I tug my shirt together and cross my arms, holding it in place. The lobby is filled with angry drunks and battered and bruised people, none of which pay attention to me as I pass by.

Phil takes me to an interrogation room located in the back of the building. The room is cold, the walls gray and uninviting. I glance up and note that Phil is watching me like he's afraid I'll spontaneously combust any second now.

"You don't have to do this," he says once again.

"No, I know. I want to do this. For Logan." This time, I manage a weak smile.

"All right," says Phil. "I'll just . . ." He points toward the double-sided mirror behind him.

I nod.

Five minutes later, he returns with another officer. "Chloe, this is Officer Rodriguez. He's going to be asking you questions."

I glance up at him, wide-eyed. "What? Where are you going?"

"To the hospital, to be with Logan."

Of course. How stupid am I? Logan might be dying on a table due to his gunshot wounds and here I am, playing the role of damsel in distress. Except, this time, Logan's not here to climb up the lattice and rescue me. I'm on my own, as is he.

"Right. Okay."

"Hi, Ms. Sullivan," says Officer Rodriguez. He sits down across from me at the table, and I wave goodbye to Phil as he closes the door behind him.

"Hi," I reply meekly.

Officer Rodriguez says, "Let's start from the beginning."

So I do. I tell him everything: from the first time Logan and I met, to the death of Jake, to the encounter Logan had with Big P in town. How Phil's reputation would have suffered if the whole town found out a police officer had a drug-addicted son. Above all else, I tell him what happened tonight, because that's what he's most interested in. By the time I'm finished, Officer Rodriguez looks more than a little shocked.

"Well," he says, "we appreciate your story. I know it's a lot to take in, and there are counselors I can recommend to you, if that's what you want."

I shake my head. "No, it's okay. I just want to forget all of this ever happened." And it's not like I can prosecute anyone;

they're all dead.

"Is there anything I can get for you? Coffee? Water?"

"Can you give me a ride?" I ask. Glancing down at my shirt, Officer Rodriguez takes the hint: I need a new top since mine was ripped.

"Sure," he says, gathering his paperwork and standing up. "I'm just going to run this to my office, and then I'll be back."

I step into the hallway as he disappears around the corner. From here, I can see the lobby, where drunks and other strange people have congregated. Some are handcuffed and chained to long rows of chairs, others are arguing with officers at the front desk. Are they in here for anything similar to what I went through? I doubt it. These look like regulars; they're too calm about their transgressions not to be.

"All set," Officer Rodriguez says, startling me. I follow him out a backdoor, where his patrol car sits in a parking lot.

Thirty minutes or so later, we pull into the driveway of the lake house. Officer Rodriguez pulls out a couple of cards from his front shirt pocket. "Here," he says, handing them to me. "One is mine, and the other is my wife's. She's a local counselor. Call either of us if you need anything, all right?"

I nod and open the passenger door. "Thanks."

Apparently, my mom has been worried about me and noticed the police car in the driveway, because she's waiting at the front door when I walk across the lawn. Her face is contorted in anxiety, and one of her hands covers her mouth.

She holds the door open for me. "Chloe, what's happened? What's going on?" One look at my shirt and her eyes fill with horror. "What the hell happened? Are you all right?"

I open my mouth to speak, but nothing comes out. Instead, I collapse into her arms and cry hysterically all over again. She pets my hair, hugs me tightly against her tiny frame, and gently shushes my out-of-control wailing.

When I finally regain my voice, I wipe away tears and say, "Oh, Mom, I have so much to tell you."

Twenty • Logan

Thoughts:

I hate bright lights.

If I'm vaguely sensing them, does this mean I've crossed over, that I'm dead?

Opening my mouth, I rasp, "Chloe."

Where is she?

Where is she?

Big P. Chloe. Gun.

It's all coming back.

Holy shit.

I don't know what's worse:

Knowing I'm dead, *knowing* I can't be there for her ever again, or narrowly escaping fatality and, as an alternative, Death trading my soul for Chloe's.

A single tear slides down the side of my face, and I can't move my arms to stop it.

Twenty-one • Chloe

I've told my mom everything. There's not a single detail I left out; no skeletons in the closet. Amazingly, she doesn't behave like I thought. Instead, she wraps her arms around me and whispers how our predicament will work out on its own, how Logan's going to pull through and live. But, most of all, she wants to meet him, even if he's on his death bed. For all I know, he might be gone already.

After I obtain a hot shower and a change of clothes, Mom grabs her purse and keys, and we pile into the trusty RAV4, traveling to the hospital. I can't believe the events over the past two hours. Everything's unfolded so quickly. One minute we were ready for the next chapter of our lives and looking forward to Logan patching up his relationship with his family, the next we were cornered and unable to run from Logan's turbulent past.

I imagine Big P and his buddies lying face down in a puddle of their blood. Do they have family and friends who will grieve their passing? If they do, are these people aware of their deaths yet? Visualizing the crime scene sectioned off with yellow tape causes a shudder to surge up my spine. Never in a million years have I thought, *Oh, yeah. I'll definitely be a part of a crime scene one day.* And now, here I am.

Mom pulls into a parking space at the hospital. Logan can't be anywhere other than ICU, so we might as well bypass the ER. They'll stick him in a room to recover after the bullets are removed . . . if he survives. Thinking about him being taken from my life causes tears to spring forth, and it takes every bit of strength left in me to push them away. I can't think like that; Logan wouldn't want me to.

"C'mon, sweetie, let's go find him," says Mom.

We enter the non-emergency side, hoping they'll have some information, but the nurse at the front desk doesn't have any new info on Logan, other than he's in surgery.

"I'll let you know when his surgery is complete. Why don't you have a seat over there?" she says, pointing toward an empty waiting area. I'm sure if this was the ER, there'd be plenty of people to sit next to. Momentarily, I wonder if that's where Phil is right now, or if they have him somewhere else in the hospital.

Hours later, the nurse at the front desk looks up from her computer and says, "They've taken him into recovery. I'll call up there and see if he's able to have visitors."

Are you kidding me? I've been here for hours and she's just now telling us we may not get to see him? I want to concurrently strangle her flabby throat and smack the bright-pink blush off her cheeks.

But, thank goodness, the heavens have opened up and spread a blessing on my mom and me, because they allow us to see Logan.

"Room 407," says the nurse. "Fourth floor, seven rooms down on the left as you exit the elevator."

Now my stomach decides to tether up. *Jeez, Chloe, it's not like the guy won't remember you.* He's probably so sedated that he won't be awake when I do show up. What I seem to be forgetting, though, is how he's made it through surgery, which sounds like he'll be okay. If he wasn't, he'd be in there much, much longer. Logan's a strong man, through, and I have utter faith in him to pull through this, just like he's pulled through his therapy with me.

The elevator dings and we step off, making quick strides down the hall. Mom opens the door to Room 407. Several nurses busy themselves around the room and pay no attention to us. Phil is bedside with Logan, holding his hand, crying. He doesn't acknowledge our presence, either.

"Let's stand outside for a minute, sweetie," Mom whispers in

199

my ear. "Give him a moment."

After five minutes or so, Phil steps into the hallway and says, "I'm going to get some fresh air and call my wife." He nods at me, and glances at my mom warily.

"Phil, this is my mom, Sandra. Mom, this is Phil, Logan's dad," I say, introducing them.

"Were you the one who saved Chloe?" Mom asks.

Phil doesn't seem put off by this question, as he replies, "If you mean, did I pull the trigger, the answer is yes."

Mom's head bobs once, almost unnoticeably. "Well, thank you. I'm forever in your debt for saving my daughter's life."

"Don't thank me, Mrs. Sullivan. You can thank whatever higher presence you believe in, because Chloe wouldn't be here right now had the young man's gun not jammed. I don't care what anyone says—she had an angel on her side." He tips his head. "Ladies, if you'll excuse me."

I watch the elevator doors close behind him. I called it luck, but maybe Phil's right, maybe my guardian angel was looking out for me. If that's true, I wish I could thank him or her.

Mom and I step into the room, and the nurses finally clear out, satisfied the IV's and machines are in place and where they should be. Logan's asleep, with tubes up his nose and in his mouth. I slide my hand underneath his and squeeze, even though I know he can't squeeze back.

"If you can hear me," I start to say, "I just wanted to tell you that I miss you already, and I'm sorry this happened." Tears bite at my eyes. *Oh, no. Not here, not now.* But I can't stop them. Tiny droplets glide down my cheeks and fall on mine and Logan's intertwined hands. I hastily wipe them away. "Anyway," I continue, calming myself, "I brought my mom to meet you."

She wraps one arm around my shoulders and holds me close. "He's adorable, Chloe."

I sniffle and laugh at the same time. "You should see his eyes; they're the most vibrant green, like the Irish countryside in springtime."

Mom hugs me tighter. "I'm sure I'll see them soon, baby."

We spend at least ten more minutes by Logan's side, and then Mom suggests we go home, eat, and get some rest. We'll be back tomorrow, but it seems too far away. I don't know what the future holds tomorrow, and that's what scares me. What if I wake up and Logan's gone? I'll never have the chance to tell him goodbye.

My stomach churns in one long sway, like the tide before a hurricane. Mom ushers me toward the door.

"I can't leave him," I say, glancing over my shoulder to Logan lying helpless and alone. "Mom, I just can't do it. He needs me right now. What if he wakes up and I'm not here? What will he think?"

"Chloe, you can't keep asking what-ifs; you just have to have faith he'll be here tomorrow. But, in the meantime, you can't run yourself down. You'll need your strength for when he does wake up." She kisses the top of my head and hugs me close.

So, I agree to go home and eat and sleep. God knows I haven't done any of the above lately. Maybe it's exactly what I need.

Twenty-two • Chloe

Mom and I arrive home, exhausted, and notice an unfamiliar car parked in the driveway; it's a four-door, blue sedan, which looks brand new.

"Who is that?" I ask.

Mom frowns. "I have no idea."

We check the car, but nobody's in it. Mom cautiously pushes on the unlocked front door, which is cracked open a few inches. "Stay back, Chloe," she whispers.

Please, Mom. Like you can stop an intruder. She was pretty handy with the baseball bat that one night, though . . .

"I'm coming with you," I whisper back, grabbing her hand

and holding on for dear life.

As we enter the living room, Dad is standing at the fireplace mantle, holding a picture frame in his hand. Slowly, he turns toward us. "Where have you two been?"

Mom straightens up. "That's none of your business."

Dad looks taken back by her reply and replaces the picture frame where it belongs. "Sandra, I hate to inform you, but it is my business. I do worry about you two, whether you choose to believe that or not."

Mom releases my hand and inches closer to Dad. "I want you out of this house. You promised you wouldn't show your face, for Chloe's sake."

"I know," he says, hanging his head. "And I'm truly sorry about what happened. You know that's not like me. All I'm asking for is a second chance, to make things right again."

I huff. "No offense, Dad, but Mom and I are doing just fine without you." Mom glances at me, surprise engraved on her face. "I don't think what you've done to us is redeemable. You've hurt Mom more times than she can count, even though she's been there for you through good times and bad, like you two swore to do when you were married. And your drinking has really gotten out of hand these last few months. What you did to me, however, was the icing on the cake. It's over and done with. Now, let us move on with our lives."

"You don't mean that, pumpkin," says Dad, his voice surging with hurt. "You can't focus on the all the terrible things

I've done. Think of the good times we've had together, as a family. Those outnumber the rest, right?"

I carefully choose my words. "Yes, they do, but sometimes the negative outweighs the positive. Besides, it's not like you've gone above and beyond to make us happy. Everything you've bought, everything you've invested in, has been for you. Mom and I weren't your family; we were assets."

"That's not tr—"

"Yes," I interrupt, "it is. You want someone who isn't a possession because you don't want to be held liable if something happens to them. You're not out for the good, Dad. You're just too greedy for that."

His lips form a thin line. Hands on hips, he looks around the room at nothing in particular. Nothing has ever really held his gaze for long, anyway. "Well," he says, "I guess this is it, then."

"I guess so," I say.

He nods a couple of times, lost in his own thoughts. "I wish you wouldn't think of me as such a monster, Chloe. Even though your mother and I aren't compatible, I had hoped we could at least work things out."

"You and Mom aren't compatible because of *you*. Plain and simple. This is your fault, and, once again, you can't even stand up and take responsibility for your actions." I snort, shaking my head. "Pathetic."

Dad's face ignites into a blaze of resentment. "You ungrateful little bitch. I've put a roof over your head, I've fed you, I've clothed you, and this is how I'm treated?"

"Don't you *dare* call her that!" Mom's face burns brightly with rage, too. "She's done nothing, and everything she's said to you is true. You wouldn't be pissed if it wasn't. You brought this on yourself, Jim, and now you'll have to find a way to crawl out—on your belly, like the snake that you are."

Dad lunges for Mom. She has a split second to decide what direction to take, but he's too quick, landing a blow to her face. She screams, and the impact causes her to fall down. I sprint forward, closing the distance between Dad and me before he hits her again. Jumping on his back, I beat his head mercilessly. Over and over again I pummel his skull, hoping I'm doing some kind of damage. If my hand and wrist are any indication, I'm going to be in a world of hurt when this is all said and done.

His hands latch on to my arms, and he hurls me off. I land on the floor with a loud *thwack*, nearly knocking me unconscious when my head slams against the hardwood. I'm barely able to ascertain Mom grabbing a vase off the entryway table and smashing it over Dad's head. This time, he's the one who's out cold.

"Chloe, baby, are you all right?" Mom squats down beside me, one hand on her face where Dad hit her, the other clutching my hand so tightly I'm losing circulation.

"Ugh." I moan. "I think so." Sitting up, I rub the back of my head. "That's gonna leave a mark."

"Help me drag him outside," Mom says, nodding toward

last summmer

Dad's unresponsive body. "If we can lock him out, he won't bother us."

"Mom, he has a key."

She crawls over to Dad, fishes around in his pockets, and pulls out his set of keys. Finding the one to the lake house, she glides it around the metal loop, until she successfully holds it in her hand. "Not anymore," she says. Standing up, we each grab one arm and drag him to the front porch, leaving his cataleptic body alone.

"I can't believe that just happened," I say once we're safely inside the house. "He's psycho even without alcohol in his system."

Mom sits down on the couch, buries her face in her hands, and sobs. Her shoulders tremble with each new cry. I wish none of this ever occurred. I wish Dad would've moved on with his life and let us live ours. Alone. Without him in it. But some things don't quite work out the way people plan.

I sit down beside her, wrapping my arms around her torso. "When we go back to Cherryview to pack," I say, "we can file a restraining order against him. He won't bother us ever again. It'll just be you and me against the world. Judging by the way we handled him, I think we're going to do just fine." I let out a short laugh to relieve tension in the room.

"That's not the man I married!" Mom wails. "That's not him."

Thirty minutes later, after consoling Mom that everything's

207

going to work out, Dad wakes up and pounds his fists against the front door. "Let me in, or I'll break in!" he bellows. Mom and I wait wordlessly, until Dad gives up. The rental car kicks up gravel as Dad backs out of the driveway, leaving in a bout of squealing tires and burnt rubber.

"We have to go to the police," Mom says, wiping away her tears.

"Let's go, then. Before he comes back."

Mom and I make it to the police station. I have to say, being here during the daytime is much different than at night. Although there are plenty of people in the lobby, they aren't the same drunken, riotous people from yesterday.

Officer Rodriguez walks around the corner, just as Mom and I make our way to the front desk. "Chloe, hey," he says. "What's going on?" He takes one look at Mom's face and his features illustrate concern. "Is that why you're here?"

"My dad," I offer. "He went crazy earlier, so we need to file a restraining order. Can you help us?"

He sighs. "Normally, we're called to the scene in cases such as this."

"Cases such as this?"

Gesturing toward my mom, he says, "Domestic assault. But there's paperwork to be filled out and sent to the court for a TPO."

"TPO?"

"Temporary Restraining Order. It lasts for three weeks, and a more permanent restraining order could take up to a month to obtain."

That's too much time. What if he comes back for us? "It's too long."

"If you want," he says, eyeing the officer behind the front desk, "I can help you obtain an Emergency Protective Order. It'll stay in effect until you obtain the TPO."

I nod frantically. "Yes! That's what we want."

"Okay. Come with me."

Officer Rodriguez sits us down in the two chairs opposite his desk, giving the full rundown of what the different restraining orders mean. I can't help but question if he would've helped had I not been molested, had he not known me. What if I hadn't gone with Logan? What if my actions and Mom's actions hadn't stopped my dad? Everything happens for a reason, people say. What if the incident with Big P happened because, somewhere in the universe, a higher being was looking out for us, knowing we'd end up right here, right now? Looking back, I wonder whether Logan would still be alive, or whether my mom and I would still be breathing. Dad could've easily lost control and killed us had Mom not stopped him.

Logan and my mom are the only people in this world who have a special place in my heart. I don't know what I'll do if I lose them. Events were set in motion over the last twenty-four hours, making me appreciate my loved ones even more. Logan has risked everything to have semblance of order in his life again, to return to his old self, and, in the process, we were lucky enough to find each other. Mom has overcome her issues with my father so she and I can get our lives back on track, so we can be together, safely. She's stronger than she realizes, I think.

Sitting here with my mom, I see a new person. Her light may have been temporarily dimmed by my father's behavior, but he never really extinguished her flame. Now more than ever, that light has sparked and improved itself. Deep in the core of my psyche, something tells me we'll be okay—finally. Dad won't harm us again, and Mom and I can move to California, away from our old, drama-filled lives.

The thing that bothers me the most is Logan, though. He's been a constant source of hope for the past two months. We hit a lot of rough patches, but we traveled past those bumps and kept moving forward. I trust my gut on this one—Logan and I will pull through this dark period in our lives, and he and I will press on like we always do.

"All set," says Officer Rodriguez. "I'll fax this over to the judge right away. If you need anything else, Mrs. Sullivan, don't hesitate to call me. Chloe has my business card, but just in case, here's an extra."

"Thank you. I won't forget this," Mom says, taking his card and dropping it in her purse.

Mom and I stand to leave, but Officer Rodriguez stops us with his final words. "Don't worry, you two. Everything will work out in the end."

I believe him.

Twenty-three • Logan

Big P laughs maniacally as he stands next to me, with B and Smooth holding me back. "It seems Ice has found a new lady." All three of them snicker together, like the fact that Ice is about to do Godknowswhat to Chloe is some big joke.

I struggle, but it's short-lived against B and Smooth; they're pretty strong. So I shout, "Don't fucking touch her!"

Big P, B, and Smooth laugh even harder at my seriously weak attempt to stop Ice from putting his hands on Chloe. She's dazed from hitting the ground so hard, and when her eyes roll around and meet mine, I yell, "Chloe, run!"

She kicks and claws at Ice, but he's just too big for her to push him off; he's too big for anybody, really. Ice's mouth moves, and Chloe looks horrified. Whatever he said to her, I'm going to cut out his fucking tongue for saying it. Then, he leans forward—so close their foreheads almost touch—and utters something else. Chloe screams, panicked, and Ice's mouth covers hers in one rapid movement.

No. *My heart pumps faster.* God, no. Stop!

Ice jerks back, and I see blood leaking from the side of Chloe's mouth. He backhands her across the face.

"Son of a bitch!" *I say through gritted teeth, fighting against B and Smooth. Big P knocks me over the back of my head, and I fall to my knees, unable to control my emotions. There's nothing I can do to help Chloe, and they're going to make me stand here and watch.*

Ice rips Chloe's shirt clean down the middle, buttons flying everywhere. She continues screaming and trying to fight him. With a couple of swift moves, Ice shoves her shorts down to her ankles. Then, the unthinkable. When I see what he does with his fingers, the way he laughs *about it, I want to vomit fireballs in his direction. I want to chop his fucking head off with a guillotine. I want to kill him. Red surrounds the edges of my vision.*

But this time around, I don't twist free of Smooth's grip when he reaches into his pocket for a cigarette. Nor do I grab his gun and shoot. No, this time, I can't free myself from their clutches. I can't summon the strength to fight them. I can't do anything, except fall to my knees and grit my teeth, as Chloe's screams carry into the night.

Chloe looks directly into my eyes when Ice presses himself on top of her, showing no more fear, and says, "It's okay, Logan. We're going to get through this, baby."

But we're not going to make it, Chloe, *I think.* They're going to be the death of us.

Twenty-four • Chloe

Logan's head writhes back and forth, and he mumbles incoherently. I lay one hand on the side of his face, hoping it'll sooth whatever nightmare he's living in.

"No," he murmurs. "No, no, no." The sound of his voice, as if he's in unforeseeable agony, tugs at my heartstrings.

I don't know if he can hear me, but I speak up anyway. "It's okay, Logan. We're going to get through this, baby."

He bursts into tears, eyes still closed, and I immediately wipe them from his face. Just seeing him this way causes an unexpected clenching of my gut, and I cry with him. Whatever horrendous dream he's having, I want to erase it from his mind.

Over the next hour, Logan is fitfully in and out of consciousness. The nurses explain that the high doses of pain medication they're pumping into his veins make him lethargic, but he should be awake soon. How soon is "soon," I'm not sure.

"Why don't you take a break, honey?" Mom says, standing up from one of the chairs in the room and walking to the end of Logan's hospital bed. "You've been here for over two hours and he hasn't awoken. We can grab some lunch and stop by later."

I shake my head. "I want to be here when he wakes up. I want to be the first thing he sees, so he knows I'm okay."

She nods, understanding. "Want me to bring you something?"

I smile. "That'd be nice."

"I think we'll join you," says Phil. He and Marcie have been quietly sitting next to my mom all morning. I don't know if they got any sleep; they've been here all night. Lucas naps on the other empty cot in the room. Marcie gently rubs his back, waking him. He's reluctant, at first, but he sits up, wiping his eyes.

"C'mon, baby. Let's get some food, okay?" she coos.

"I don't wanna," he says. His hair sticks straight up at the crown of his head. "I want to stay with Logan."

"Logan's sleeping. He needs his rest."

"Mama," he says, looking up at her as he slides off the bed, "is Logan going to be sick forever?" Phil and Marcie explained to Lucas last night that Logan was ill. They didn't want to frighten the poor kid with what really happened to his brother.

216

She laughs kindly. "No, baby. He's not. But we have to leave him alone for a little while so he can get better."

"Okay," he says, satisfied with her response. He turns toward me. "Are you going to watch over him, Chloe?"

"Yep," I reply.

He nods his head once, swiftly. "'Kay." As he and the rest of the family exit, I hear him ask, "Can we go to McDonald's?"

Marcie laughs. "Whatever you want, sweetie."

Mom follows them closely, closing the door behind her, but not before she winks at me. Whatever that's for.

Ten to fifteen minutes later, Logan begins mumbling again, his head twisting back and forth. "Chloe," I hear him say. "*Chloe.*"

"I'm here, baby. I'm here." I squeeze his hand and resume caressing his face with my other.

Leisurely, he opens his eyes and blinks a few times, as he figures out where he is. He squints at the fluorescent lighting and groans. Licking his lips, he gulps once, his Adam's apple bobbing. "Chloe," he rasps, gradually turning his head to face me.

Oh, thank God! I might seriously scream from excitement right now.

"I'm here, Logan. I'm here. You're safe."

"I'm . . . alive?"

Fresh tears puddle in my eyes, and I can't stop them from rolling down my cheeks. "Yes," I say, nearly choking on my sobs. "Yes, baby, you're alive."

He moans and rubs his face with his other hand. "I thought I'd never see you again."

"*You?* I thought I was the one who'd never see you again."

He swallows hard. "Big P . . . is he?"

"He's dead."

Tension leaves Logan's body. "Good. I'm glad we've seen the last of him." He looks at me then, panic hitting him. "Did he do anything to you?"

I know he's thinking about Ice, about what a close call that was. "No," I say, shaking my head. "Nothing like that, anyway."

Logan grips my hand tighter. "What'd he do?"

"Does it matter? I'm here. You're here. We're together again, miraculously."

"I want to know," he presses.

Squeezing my eyes shut, I remember the gun aimed at my head, the determination in Big P's eyes. When I visualize him pulling the trigger, I recoil.

"Chloe?" Logan's voice drags me out of my reverie. "What'd he do? Tell me." He tugs at our entwined fingers, and keeps tugging until I crawl onto the bed, lying by his side, head resting against his chest.

"He pointed the gun at me, pulled the trigger, and . . . it jammed."

Logan flinches. "What?"

"Your dad shot him," I add, as if that might lighten the

moment.

"He pulled the fucking—" Logan's jaw clenches as he grinds his teeth in annoyance. "If he weren't dead already, I swear to God I'd kill him myself. I should've when I had the chance."

Lightly, I graze my fingertips over his jaw line and watch his muscles relax. "Ssh. Enough of that. No more thoughts of killing anybody. No more fighting. No more wasting away on hate. Got it?"

He gives me a sidelong glance, then mumbles, "Yeah. Got it."

"It's over. It's done with. Let the past be the past. We can't change any of it, and in a way, I wouldn't want to, because we both made it out. Alive."

Shaking his head in agitation, he says, "I can't believe he—"

I place my index finger over his lips, silencing him. "Shut up and kiss me."

He obliges as I rise up, carefully brushing his mouth over mine, slowly tracing my lips with his tongue. He intensifies the kiss as I roll over, on top of him. Both of our mouths move in a measured, agonizing rhythm, and I feel as if my heart will fly out of my chest. Logan cradles my head with one hand, and tilts my chin up even more with the other. With my neck outstretched, he breaks away and trails soft kisses across my skin. Lower, lower, lower. God, I want him to go lower, but he stops just above the hemline of my shirt.

Lifting his head to glance at me, he smirks and says, "We'll

219

continue this later."

I hoarsely respond, "Okay."

He chuckles. "You might want to hop down in case one of the nurses comes in here and catches you in my bed." He kisses my forehead. "I wouldn't want them to kick you out of here."

I slide off the side, a little put out. He's right, though. These beds were made for one patient and one patient *only*.

"Plus, our parents will be back soon, with food," I add.

Logan's stomach growls in response, and he rubs it. "I could use some food."

"Sounds like it."

"I could use you, too," he says, with a mischievous glint in his eyes.

I try not to grin. "I think you need food even more."

"I don't think so," he says, his voice dropping an octave; it's throaty and gruff and I'm doing everything I can *not* to jump back in bed with him. I think he feels the same way, because he doesn't break eye contact with me for a second. There's an electrical charge in the room, one that wasn't there before. "Chloe . . ."

"Yeah?" I squeak.

He extends one hand, and I take it in mine. "Chloe, there's something I've wanted to say for a while, but I was too chicken shit to admit it to myself, let alone say it out loud."

My throat dries up, like the heat from the sun outside has found its way through the hospital window and sucked away the fluid in my mouth. Wide-eyed, I feel as if my eyeballs might escape from their sockets. I know what he's about to say; I just can't believe he's going to really say it.

"I love you," he blurts, throwing his head backward against the stack of pillows behind him and sighing. "I think I would love you even if we never met. If we lived separate lives in some alternate reality, where I was never homeless or a drug addict, I would've never truly been happy, because all the other girls in that world wouldn't have been you."

He clutches my hand with such strength, it's as if he's afraid I'll slip away. "I think I would've searched for you, even though I wouldn't have known what I was searching for. But I like to think that, when I found you, I'd be like a blind person seeing for the first time. The world would open up, be colorful, magical, and infinite—and I would conquer it all, as long as I could have you."

I can't see through my tears. "I love you, too," are the only words I can push out of my throat.

"Come here," he whispers, pulling me closer to the edge of the bed. I lean over and lay my head on his chest. For a while, the only present sounds are that of my sobs and his heartbeat thrumming against my ear. "We're going to get through this," he says, now taking on the role of emotional supporter, which is what I've been for the last two months.

"Yes, we are," I agree, wiping away the last of my tears. "But first, you need to rest up."

"For what? I've been resting."

I smirk. "For that sensational, over-the-moon girlfriend of yours, named Chloe. I heard she's made of awesomesauce."

"I heard she's the icing to my cake."

"The butter to your bread, too?"

Logan attempts to hide his grin. "The banana to my split."

I giggle. "That doesn't even make sense."

"Okay, fine, then," he says, pretending to be offended. "I heard she's the apple to my apple tree, the hamburger bun to my hamburger patty—"

"Oh, my God." I burst into laughter. "Why are all of the comparisons food-related?"

Logan raises one eyebrow. "Probably because I'm hungry."

"Mom's bringing me some food, so you can have mine."

"But until then . . ." Logan trails off, pinning me with his eyes.

I shake my head. "Until then, you get some rest."

"How about we just make out instead?" One corner of his mouth curves into a wicked leer.

"It wouldn't surprise me, Logan Andrews, if you said you wanted to make out, but then you had something else in mind."

He presses one hand over his heart, faking insult. "Chloe Sullivan, you offend me. I would never taint the good graces of a lady."

I begin tugging on the privacy curtain around the bed, the metal clinking as it gradually closes us in, creating a thin veil between us and the outside. "Too bad I'm not much of a lady. Besides, your muscles haven't been limbered up for a couple of days. Don't you think it's time we fix that?"

Epilogue

One Year Later

"Is that the last of them, babe?" I ask.

Logan carries five grocery bags on each arm, setting them on the counter. He nods. "Yep. That's it."

"Our first groceries," I say with a smile.

He kisses the side of my head as he slides both arms around my waist. With his forehead pressed against mine, he admits, "I have a feeling there will be many more firsts with you."

"Mmm. I think you might be right."

"Of course I am," he says, pulling away to help me sort through five-hundred-dollars worth of food and household items.

Since the move to California with my mom, Logan and I stayed in touch, making a point to speak to each other every day, at least once. But that was never really enough. Three months later, Logan came to visit for a couple of weeks, decided he liked California, and planned on moving once he found a job and a place to live. Eight months after that, he found both: a job at a local rehabilitation center, counseling those who are trying to cope with their addiction, and, as for a place to live, well, he found that with me. We signed the rental agreement just last week. The place is undecorated, but we decided we'll furniture shop this weekend. Food, however, was a must.

"So I've been thinking," I begin, glancing over our kitchen bar to the naked living room. "What if we get a purple couch? Or blue? I like blue; it'd go with the beach vibe around here. Then we can hang some mementos on the wall, maybe a few pictures of us."

Deadpan, Logan says, "Um, babe? Just because we live near a beach doesn't mean we have to decorate the place with seashells and mermaids."

I shrug. "It's just an idea. What about a yellow theme? Yellow reminds me of the sun."

"Chloe . . ."

"Or maybe a mixture of burnt orange and hot pink, like a sunset."

"I swear to God, if you start decorating in that pink frilly shit, I'll throw it out the window."

I gasp dramatically, pretending to be offended. "You wouldn't dare!"

Logan cracks a smile. "You already know the answer to that."

We were lucky enough to find an apartment only a few blocks from the beach, though it's a little on the pricey side. But we'll manage.

"So I've been thinking . . ." Logan mimics.

I roll my eyes. "What is it?"

"Hang out at the beach until it gets dark?" His face lights up when he talks about the ocean, like he's seven years old again. "Pleeease?"

"Okay." I scan our tiny kitchen. "We can't exactly bring drinks or food with us, though."

He tucks a strand of hair behind my ear. "That's fine. I'll cook us something when we get back. I just want to enjoy another sunset with you."

My cheeks ache from beaming. "Sometimes you're the cutest romantic I know, and other times I still want to punch you like I did the second time we met."

He throws his head back, laughing. "I'm surprised you haven't hit me again."

Narrowing my eyes and holding up my fist, I say, "I only reserve this for pissed-off moments."

"Trust me, I know," he says, rubbing his face at the memory of the time I hit him in the cottage.

"But I highly doubt we'll have one of those moments again," I concede. "You're not as much of an asshole as you were back then." I stick my tongue out.

His eyebrows cinch and his features lose amusement, like he's falling into one of his dark places again. "No, I'm not."

My hands instinctively move to cup his face. "I'm sorry. I didn't mean—"

"No, it's okay."

"No, it's not. I'm sorry. I shouldn't say things like that."

Months ago, we had a minor setback when we hit the town one night to eat dinner and there was a homeless man quietly sitting nearby. One glance at him and Logan relapsed into his shadowy space. It took me almost a week to pull him out of that void, and it's taken even longer to convince him he won't ever live that way again; at least, not if I'm around to see my promise through of staying with him forever. I don't think Logan will ever fully recover from what he's lived through, but he's better off than he was, and he has a small network of family and friends who will support him.

"Let's go to the beach."

"'Kay," he murmurs.

I stand on my tiptoes and kiss him. As I pull back, his hands grip my waist, rendering me unable to move. His leans in and his lips cover mine, igniting a gradual ache in my body. The kiss deepens, becomes forceful, even, as if he's claiming what's his. Even after all this time, I'm still surprised at the adoration I feel for Logan. I admire him on so many levels; the closeness he has to his family and his brother, respect for manning up and overcoming his drug addiction, and the affection he displays to me each and every day.

He severs our connection. "God, I love you," he says, kissing my nose, forehead, cheeks, and lips again.

"I love you, too," I murmur against his mouth.

"Now we can go to the beach." He grins.

I wink at him as I saunter by, grabbing my purse and keys off the counter.

There aren't too many people soaking up the sun, sand, and surf at this hour. Within a couple of weeks, they'll be out in full force. Logan and I find a quieter spot amid the rows of lawn chairs, sandcastles, and colorful towels. On the horizon, the sun relaxes, providing spectators with the illusion of sinking into the ocean. Half of the bright sphere has already disappeared; the other half is hanging out, either sad it's leaving until tomorrow or extending the moment for us all. I haven't decided which.

Logan stands behind me, wrapping his arms around my shoulders. "I'd be dead if it weren't for you. You know that, right?" he whispers in my ear.

Despite the warm weather, I shiver. "Logan . . ."

"I'm serious."

"Yes," I say, "I know."

"And you know I'd do anything for you."

"Yes, I know that, too."

"I don't want us to ever be apart," he says, squeezing me tighter against him.

I turn around in his arms. "Where's this coming from?"

His brows furrow as he glances over every inch of my face. Dropping to one knee in the sand, he reaches into the pocket of his board shorts and pulls out a tiny, black box. "Chloe Sullivan, will you marry me?" He pops open the small box, revealing a glistening diamond ring. The center diamond is larger than the row of other diamonds beside it.

My eyes widen and I gasp. "Logan—"

"You're my lifesaver, Chloe," he interrupts. "When I was drowning, you rescued me. I won't ever forget what you did." He grabs one of my hands and brushes his thumb over my skin, sending another shiver through my body. "I can't live without you."

I close my eyes. Is this really happening? Did he really just ask me to spend the rest of my life with him? I mean, we've already been together for a year and stuck it out through some crazy times. What else will life throw at us?

"Just think about it," he adds. "You don't have to—"

"Okay," I say decisively. "I'll marry you."

"Yes?" A hesitant grin appears, like he can't believe I'm agreeing. Like my brave, sweet Logan was terrified I would've turned him down.

"YES!" I squeal. "A thousand times, yes!"

He laughs and picks me up, wheeling me around in circles as

he kisses every inch of my face. Sometimes, in seconds like this, I imagine it's just him and me, all alone on our private island, hidden from the rest of the world. I imagine, once upon a time, we had normal lives, and our families met on the lake: Logan's parents on their imaginary boat, and Dad taking ours on the water like he used to. I imagine Mom and Dad happy and in love like they were twenty years ago, socializing with Phil and Marcie, while Logan and I jet-ski with Lucas. I imagine Logan wasn't a homeless heroin addict; he was still an all-star on the football field, who didn't require morphine to dull the pain of his shoulder injury. I imagine Jessica and I were still best friends, and that her father was never tragically killed.

But the truth of the matter is fate brought us together under different circumstances, circumstances Logan's still not proud of. With time, though, he'll overcome his demons, and I'll be there to support him every step of the way. Although, years from now, when people ask us our secret, I'll tell them the truth: where it all began and what we went through together. How we managed to move mountains just to get where we are right now. But, most of all, how it was the best and worst summer of our lives.

ABOUT THE AUTHOR

Rebecca Rogers expressed her creative side at an early age and hasn't stopped since. She won't hesitate to tell you that she lives inside her imagination, and it's better than reality.

To stay up to date with Rebecca's latest books, check out her website at www.rebeccaarogers.com or find her on social sites such as Goodreads, Facebook, and Twitter.

CPSIA information can be obtained
at www.ICGtesting.com
Printed in the USA
LVOW04s1826021116
511368LV00009B/1008/P